ALICE MATTHEWS—Her passion for Steven Frame would burn in her heart forever. Hopelessly devoted, she would never allow herself to love another man.

STEVEN FRAME—His desperate pursuit of Alice became an obsession. He refused to accept the notion that he would never again hold her in his arms.

RACHEL MATTHEWS—Her evil schemes hurt the people she claimed to love the most. The only person Rachel truly loved was herself . . . and the only thing that mattered to her was having it all.

———————————

Series Story Editor **Mary Ann Cooper** is America's foremost soap opera expert. She writes the nationally syndicated column *Speaking of Soaps*, is a major contributor to soap opera magazines, and has appeared as a guest on numerous radio and television talk shows.

Martha Winslow, author of *Caress from the Past*, is a renowned novelist and television writer who currently resides in New York City.

Dear Friend,

If Alice Matthews has one fatal flaw, it is that she walks away from a confrontation. Rachel counted on that when she plotted to steal Steven Frame away from her.

In book 5 of the ANOTHER WORLD series, Alice begins to realize that you can't run away from the past. At Pioneer Communications Network Inc., we relish this history. Our Soaps & Serials paperback books give you the opportunity to savor the rich past of soap opera stories from your favorite shows. Relive the greatest moments of soap opera drama with Soaps & Serials books.

For Soaps & Serials books,

Mary Ann Cooper

Mary Ann Cooper

P.S. If you missed previous volumes of the ANOTHER WORLD books and can't find them in your local book source, please see the order form inserted in the back of this book.

ANOTHER WORLD

5
CARESS FROM THE PAST

Soaps™ & Serials

PIONEER COMMUNICATIONS NETWORK, INC.

Caress from the Past

ANOTHER WORLD paperback novels are published and distributed by Pioneer Communications Network, Inc.

SOAPS & SERIALS™ is a trademark of Pioneer Communications Network, Inc.

ISBN: 0-916217-35-3

Printed in the United States of America

10 9 8 7 6 5 4 3 2 1

5

CARESS FROM THE PAST

Chapter One
Rachel's Escape

With mixed emotions Steven Frame pressed the doorbell of the stately country house, causing the chimes to sound off in their crisp, euphoric tones. So much love and care had gone into this house long ago when he'd had it built for his beloved Alice. The place still dredged up some of Steve's deepest sentiments. But now that Rachel had taken up residence here, the mansion had become an enemy camp, an empty shell of a home.

Steve punched the doorbell again and turned his collar up to ward off the bitter January wind. Yet his fleece-lined jacket did nothing to warm the icy grip of disappointment that had overcome him recently. He'd discovered that his marriage to Rachel was a farce. She had viciously manipulated him—blatantly tricked him. And as a result, he'd nearly lost Alice . . . sweet, innocent Alice.

"Steven, darling!" Rachel's eyes widened with calculated delight when she threw open the door and found him standing on the front porch. "Please, come in. You must be freezing to death!" She reached toward him, inviting him into the spacious vestibule.

Steve stepped inside, but proceeded no further than the front foyer, where he firmly planted his feet and shoved his hands into the pockets of his jacket. "I've come for Jamie," he explained, skipping the meaningless pleasantries. "We're spending the afternoon together."

"Oh, Steven, that's quite impossible," Rachel said, feigning innocence. "Jamie's off with my mother this afternoon." An extremely attractive woman with dark hair and a heart-shaped face, Rachel had turned many a man's head. Yet Steve couldn't help thinking how out of place she looked here in this house, the house she had totally redecorated in a desperate and unsuccessful attempt to blot out the memory of Alice.

He pierced her with a dark, brooding stare. "You can't do this to me, Rachel!"

"Can't I?" she sniffed. "I'm Jamie's mother. I decide where he goes and what he does. *And* who he sees."

"You can't keep him from seeing his own father," Steve growled.

She sniffed again. "If Jamie's own father really wanted to see his son, he wouldn't have moved out of the house his son is living in."

"That's beside the point."

She shrugged. "That's what you say."

"All right, Rachel." Steve had barely come into the house, and now he turned to leave. "You've kept me from seeing Jamie this afternoon, but I'm warning you now not to try it again."

"Big talk," she snapped. "I'll do as I please about Jamie, and there's nothing you can do to stop me."

Suddenly Steve grabbed her by the wrist. "Now you

listen to me, Rachel. You trapped me into marrying you by using Jamie, and now you're trying to hang on to me by using him, but it's not going to work. As Jamie's father I have rights, and if I have to go to court to get those rights spelled out for you, I will."

She pulled away from him. "I have a lawyer now."

"Good. How do you expect to pay him?"

Rachel frowned. "What do you mean?"

"Just what I said, Rachel. How do you expect to pay him? Where will you get the money?"

"Where I always get the money I need. From our account at the bank."

"And who puts the money into that account, Rachel?"

Not noted for her mental accomplishments, Rachel began to understand now what he had been getting at. "You can't take that account away from me."

His dark eyes bored into her. "You try any more tricks with Jamie, and we'll see what I can and can't do."

"That's blackmail."

"No, Rachel, not blackmail. Tit for tat. I'll be here next Tuesday afternoon at three o'clock to pick up Jamie. See that he's here and ready for me."

Rachel's mother, Ada, had a much younger brother named Sam Lucas. After a bad start in life, including a jail term, Sam had straightened out, studied law, worked for John Randolph, and now lived and practiced law in the nearby town of Somerset. A big, burly, gentle man with dark hair and dark eyes, he had agreed to be Rachel's lawyer, a decision he was to regret many times over, starting with the morning he went out to her house to see her after she had been served with a summons announcing that a suit for divorce was being filed against her.

When she showed it to him he shrugged and said, "Why don't you let him have it, Rachel?"

That was like asking Mount Etna to erupt. She stamped her foot and screamed at him. "You're no different from anybody else! You're supposed to be on my side. You said you would represent me. You call this representing me? You've been to Steve, haven't you? You've made a deal with him, haven't you? That's a dirty double-crossing thing to try, Sam, but you're not going to get away with it, because I'll—"

He had been staring at her in disbelief and horror. Now he yelled at her to stop, and when she finally did, he said, "Now hold on a minute, will you? I haven't been to Steve. I haven't made any deals. The only person I've talked to is John Randolph, and that was lawyer to lawyer. I only suggested you let Steve have the divorce because he wants it. What's the point in trying to stay married to somebody who doesn't want you anymore?"

Rachel raised her chin in her familiar gesture of defiance. "Steve only *thinks* he doesn't want me anymore. But he'll come back to me. I know he will."

Hands on his hips, shaking his dark head, Sam said, "How do you know that?" Before she could erupt again he held up one of his hands. "And don't jump down my throat now, Rachel. I'm just trying to work my way through to some understanding of your situation."

"My 'situation,'" Rachel said, picking up the word from him and speaking fiercely, "is that I could make Steve happy again—the way I made him happy before— if only everybody would leave us alone."

Rachel had poured out her tirade against Sam in the big foyer of the country house. Now he walked into the living room, trying to gain time to think, and she followed him. "I'm afraid everybody isn't going to leave you alone," he said, "and unfortunately, that everybody includes Steve Frame." Sam walked to the fireplace and turned to face her. "Look, Rachel. I can get you a nice big settlement. You'll have security, freedom."

She flung herself down on the sofa facing the fireplace. "I don't want freedom. I want things to stay the way they are."

"With you living out here in the country in this big house all by yourself?"

"You're no better than John Randolph."

Sam shook his head. "I wish I were half as good as he is. Rachel, being emotional about this isn't going to resolve anything. Now, as far as the suit is concerned—"

"They haven't got a suit," she said, cutting him off. "What my father did he did on his own, without my knowing anything about it. And that's what he'll testify to."

Sam shrugged. "All right. Fine. So we win the suit. What then?"

She frowned at him. "What do you mean, what then?"

A fire was burning in the fireplace behind Sam, and the heat was beginning to feel uncomfortable. He moved away from the fireplace and sat down in an armchair near the sofa. "Do you think Steve will come back here to live with you, everything forgiven and forgotten?"

"I haven't done anything to be forgiven for."

Too restless to sit, Sam got up again and paced up and down the room. "Rachel, we're going around in circles. What I'm trying to say is, if you refuse to give Steve a divorce, and he can't win one from you, you're still going to end up losing him. He's not going to come back to you."

"That may be," Rachel said, "but at least he won't be able to marry Alice—not as long as he's married to me."

Sam stopped pacing and came to stand before her, looking down at her. "So that's what it comes down to?"

She looked up at him and nodded, her face set. "That's exactly what it comes down to."

For all her firmness of purpose, Rachel was beginning to panic. After her session with Sam, she went to John Randolph and railed at him over Steve's threats to cut off her money supply, making a threat of her own—that if Steve did win his suit against her she would take Jamie away from him forever. A few days later Steve took Jamie to see his sister Janice's new apartment, the one she now shared with Alice, and Janice gave Jamie a picture of his paternal grandmother. When Rachel saw it she believed Janice was trying to take Jamie away from her and went storming into town to have it out with her. Noboby had told her Alice was living there too, and when Alice answered the door, Rachel stared at her in disbelief. "What are you doing here?" Rachel demanded.

"I live here, Rachel," Alice said. "What are you doing here?"

Alice's cool blond beauty, her inner strength that gave the lie to her look of Dresden-china fragility, had always put Rachel off, and it put her off now. Backing away, looking up and down the hall, she said, "Maybe I have the wrong apartment."

Alice didn't move. "What do you want, Rachel?"

"I want to see Janice."

"Then you don't have the wrong apartment." Turning, she called out, "Janice! Rachel is here to see you."

Janice came to the doorway, and Alice went back into the apartment. A somewhat plain young woman, Janice had some of her brother's features, but she lacked his magnetic charm. Originally an ally of Rachel's, she had become Alice's friend now.

Rachel was now staring at Janice in disbelief. "You live here with Alice?"

Janice nodded. "Yes."

"With Alice?" Rachel said again, still disbelieving.

"Yes, Rachel. With Alice."

Rachel took a breath and let it out, a hard look settling on her face. "How could you do that to me? How could you?" Before Janice could say anything, Rachel shook her dark head. "No. Don't bother to answer, Janice. You're just like everybody else. That's what I was coming here to tell you—without even knowing about you and Alice." She took the picture out of her purse and threw it on the floor at Janice's feet. "There. You can have that back. And this time keep it. You may think you can take Jamie away from me with little tricks like that, but it's not going to work, Janice, any more than Alice is going to accomplish anything trying to take Jamie's father away from me."

With that Rachel left and went straight to the hotel room, where Sam was staying while he was in Bay City. He sat at a makeshift desk, working on some legal papers, wearing the green eyeshade he always wore when he worked. Opening the door to her, he took the eyeshade off and waved her to the room's one armchair.

He returned to the straight chair he'd been sitting in before, turning the chair around to face her. "Now what?" he said, as he sat down, not knowing what to expect but figuring from the look on Rachel's face that it was something momentous.

"Did you know Alice is living with Steve's sister?"

"No, I didn't, but so what?"

She stared at him. "So what? Don't you see what Alice is up to?"

Sam shook his head. "No, I don't. But I'm confident you'll tell me, Rachel."

His small attempt at humor was lost on her. "You bet I will," she said. "I bet Alice and Steve are having an affair, and that's where they meet to have it—in that apartment she shares with Janice."

"It's possible," Sam said judiciously. "But it doesn't sound like Alice. Or Steve either, for that matter."

"That's right," Rachel retorted bitterly. "Stick up for them. Never mind that you're *my* lawyer, not theirs."

Sam lifted his hands in a gesture of futility. "I'm not sticking up for them, Rachel. I was just making an observation, that's all."

She made a dismissing face. "You think Alice is too goody-goody to have an affair. Well, she's not. She had one for months with Eliot Carrington—that newspaper columnist she went to work for when she ran out on Steve." Alice had taken care of Eliot's young son, Dennis, who had had a congenital heart defect that was finally corrected by Alice's cardiologist brother, Russ.

"How do you know that?" Sam asked.

"I just know it, that's all."

He shook his head. "The same way you now know she's having an affair with Steve?"

With an impatient gesture Rachel got up from the armchair and went to stand at the room's one window, looking out at an air shaft. "Oh, what's the good of talking to you," she complained. "I should have saved my breath."

"You're not using your head, Rachel."

She turned from the window to frown at him. "What's my head got to do with it?"

He sighed. "Steve wants to divorce you, right? So he can marry Alice."

"So he claims."

"And he's having a hard enough time doing that without putting himself in further jeopardy."

Her frown deepened. "Don't talk to me in all that legal gibberish, Sam. Use words I can understand."

He sighed again. "'Jeopardy' is an ordinary word, Rachel, but never mind. What I'm trying to say is, Steve isn't going to do anything that will make getting a divorce from you any harder than it already is."

Rachel was still frowning. "You mean having an affair with Alice would do that—make it harder for him to get a divorce? How, Sam?" Her frown had vanished. In its place was an eager look. "Tell me how."

"Well, look at it from his point of view. For all Steve knows, you might sue Alice for alienation of affections. You're not going to, of course, but—"

She cut in on him. "What do you mean I'm not going to? I haven't said anything one way or the other. You mean if I sue Alice for alie—uh—whatever you said, I could stop Steve from getting a divorce from me?"

Sam was already sorry he'd put the idea in her head, and now he tried to talk her out of it. "You'd have to win the suit first, Rachel, and then it's no flat-out guarantee."

Rachel had always been the type to hear only what she wanted to hear. Ignoring the last part of his remark, she said, "But suppose I did win it."

"Before you start supposing that," Sam said, still trying to talk her out of it, "consider what you'd have to do to win. You'd have to prove that Steve and Alice are in fact having an affair."

Rachel left her place at the window and came back to sit in the armchair. "So? I could prove that."

"How?"

There was a glint in her dark eyes. "I'll find a way."

"That's not good enough," Sam said with a shake of his head. "I'm sorry I brought it up, Rachel. And I didn't bring it up to put ideas in your head, but only to demonstrate why I think Steve and Alice are bending over backward not to break any rules or any laws."

Rachel didn't like being opposed. She gave Sam a sulky look. "I don't know why what I think isn't as good as what you think. I'll just have to get some proof, that's all."

Sam put up his hands in self-defense. "Don't come to me looking for that, Rachel. I'm your lawyer, not a private eye."

"I didn't say anything about coming to you. I'll do it myself. I've been wanting to get out of that big white elephant anyhow."

He frowned at her. "What are you talking about?"

"The house. I'm sick of being stuck way out there in the country with nobody to talk to except Jamie. I'm going to sell the house and get an apartment here in town."

Sam shook his head. She was impossible. "Rachel, you can't sell that house."

She glared at him. "I'd like to know why not."

"Because it's not yours to sell, that's why not."

"Oh," she said. "Well, then, get Steve to sell it."

"Oh, sure." Sam folded his arms across his chest. "Easy assignment number three-oh-two. 'Hello there, Steve. Rachel wants you to sell the house so she can take an apartment in town, the better to keep an eye on you and Alice and what the two of you might it be up to. You'll do it, you say? I knew I could count on you, Steve. Thanks a lot.'" Sam shook his head again. "Come on, Rachel."

Rachel gave him an exasperated look. "If you're through clowning, Sam. . . . You talk about me not using my head. You're not using yours. Tell Steve—or John, or whoever you talk to—that I want to move to an apartment to be near Jamie's school. Steve will do anything for Jamie."

"Including selling the house he built for Alice?" Before she could say anything he raised his hands again in that same gesture of self-defense. "All right, Rachel, all right, all right. I'll ask him. But don't expect a yes answer."

The next day Sam went to John Randolph's office to make his request for Rachel. Steve was there conferring with John about a business deal, so Sam made the appeal to both of them. Steve's reaction was just about what Sam had expected. "Is she kidding?" he said, incredulous.

Sam concentrated on keeping a straight face. "No. She wants to be nearer Jamie's school."

"What she wants," Steve said, getting up from his chair in front of John's desk and walking to the window to stare down at the street below, "is not to be stuck out there in the country all by herself. Well, I've told her before she's free to leave. And she still is. But I'm not selling the house, or paying for an apartment for her, either."

From his chair before the desk, Sam addressed Steve's back. "I told Rachel I didn't think you'd be willing to sell the house. But I think you ought to give some thought to letting her move to an apartment. For one thing, it would make it easier for you to see Jamie. And for another, it would make her more reasonable about letting you see him."

Steve turned from the window to look at Sam. "I've already told Rachel that if she plays any more tricks with me where Jamie's concerned, I'll cut off her support. And I will, too."

The two lawyers exchanged looks. Then Sam turned back to Steve to say, "And cut off Jamie's support as well?"

Steve frowned at him. "Jamie has a trust fund."

"A trust fund doesn't give him a place to live. And anyhow, Steve, how is it going to look to a little kid like Jamie if you cut off his mother's support—a man with all your money? You don't want to come out of all this having a son who won't have anything to do with you, do you?"

John had been sitting behind his desk, quietly listening to Sam and Steve. Now he stepped in, saying, "Sam, let Steve and me talk this over between us, and then I'll get back to you on it. Okay?"

"Sure," Sam said. "That's fine with me."

John showed Sam out of the office, then came back and sat down again at his desk, motioning Steve back to his seat across from him. "I had the feeling you were about to explode, Steve, and, well . . . I don't like saying this, but I think Sam's right. About the apartment and Jamie, I mean."

Steve *had* been about to explode, and now he did. He slammed a hand down on John's desk. "Damn her! It's one trick after another. And the way she uses Jamie to get what she wants. Why doesn't anybody worry about that and what effect it might have on the boy? Why is it only what *I* do or don't do that will look bad to Jamie?"

"I know," John said sympathetically, "but Jamie's too young to understand the subtleties, Steve."

Steve settled back in his chair with a tired sigh. "Oh, all right. Let her have an apartment. I'd just as soon have her out of the house anyhow. I never wanted her to live there in the first place. And she only wanted to live there to spite Alice. She's never liked the house, or the location."

"That's right," John agreed. He had seen for himself how Rachel hated the house. "And maybe the move into town will improve her mood. She might be more willing to listen to reason."

"Maybe," Steve said, "but I doubt it." He stood up and shoved his hands into his pants pockets. "In any case, what do we care whether or not she's willing to listen to reason? Once the judge rules in our favor we're finished with her. And that can't be soon enough for me." He picked up his briefcase and walked to the closet where he'd hung his coat.

From his desk John gave him a concerned look. "Don't pocket the decision, Steve, until it's in your hand."

Steve turned back to him, frowning. "You're not having second thoughts, are you?"

"No. I wouldn't have filed the suit if I didn't think I could win it." He folded his hands. "But I never count on anything until it's done. Maybe it's just being superstitious, but . . ." John shrugged and left the sentence unfinished.

Steve stood there looking at him, a cold shiver of fear going through him. There was no way he was going to lose his suit to divorce Rachel. No way. No matter what.

Chapter Two

Just a Kiss

In doubting that the move to town would improve Rachel's mood or make her more willing to listen to reason, Steve was right on target. She was as intractable as ever—and still looking for evidence that Steve and Alice were having an affair.

One afternoon toward the end of January they seemed to give it to her.

After getting off duty at the hospital, Alice stopped on her way home to see her childhood friend Lenore Curtin, whose husband Walter had been killed some years earlier in a tragedy that still haunted many Bay City residents. Some time after the accident, Lenore, left with an infant son, went to work for Steve Frame as an architectural consultant, a position she still held.

She hadn't been home long herself when the doorbell rang, and she opened the door. "Alice, how nice to see you. Come in, come in, before you freeze."

"It is a bit brisk out," Alice said, stepping inside.

Lenore closed the door and held out her hands for

Alice's navy blue wool cloak that she wore over her white nurse's uniform. A tall, well-proportioned young woman, Lenore had blue eyes and tawny hair worn shoulder length. And she had a handsome face and an elegant bearing that made her the envy of many of her peers, including Rachel, who had tried for a long time without success to become a friend and confidante of Lenore's.

Lenore smiled now at her lifelong friend. "I don't like telling you this, Alice, but if I don't you'll be upset at me."

Alice frowned. "What's happened now?"

Lenore shook her head. "Nothing's happened. It's just that Steve is coming by here in a little while. He's bringing Jamie over to play with Wally, and I thought maybe you wouldn't want to be here when they came."

Alice reached out for the cloak she had just handed over. "You thought right, Lenore. Give me my cloak and I'll grab my broom and sail on out of here."

The words were scarcely out of her mouth when the doorbell rang.

"Oh-oh," Alice said. "Me and my magic timing."

"It might be somebody else," Lenore said, but when she opened the door there were Steve and Jamie on the stoop. "Come in," she said to Steve. "I have all kinds of company today. How are you, Jamie?"

"Fine, thanks, Mrs. Curtin," the little seven-year-old said, walking in ahead of his father. "Oh," he said when he saw Alice. "I remember you." He smiled at her. "You make terrific chocolate-chip cookies."

Alice smiled back at him. "I'm glad you remember them, Jamie, and me as well. You've grown a lot."

"I know." His smile broadened. "My dad says it's one of the things I do best."

"Hi, Alice," his father said, following the boy into the house. "What a nice surprise." Steve grinned.

"For me too," she said. "I didn't know Lenore was expecting you."

"Jamie," Lenore said, "Wally's upstairs in his room waiting for you to help him set up his new electric train set. Do you want to go on up?"

"Sure." He turned to his father. "Do you want to too, Daddy?"

"You go on up, son, and I'll be up in a few minutes."

"Okay." Jamie turned to Alice and smiled at her again. "I hope I'll see you here again sometime."

She returned his smile. "Me, too, Jamie."

The three adults watched as he went upstairs.

"Well," Lenore said, turning to Steve and Alice, "I'm going out to the kitchen to fix a snack for the boys. I'll leave you to your own resources."

"I'm not staying, Lenore," Alice said to her friend's departing back.

"Can't you stay even a minute, Alice?" Steve asked, the ache to touch her, to kiss her, to hold her in his arms welling up in him.

"Darling," she answered, "I'd like to stay right here with you forever, but I don't think it would be very smart of me to do it."

Steve sighed. "No. I suppose not. But don't go without telling me how you are."

She smiled radiantly at him. "Darling, I'm fine. I couldn't be better." Then, slowly, she shook her head. "Well, that's not true. I could be better if—well, you know."

"Yes, I know," he agreed. "And it isn't *if.* It's *when.*"

"I hope so," she said with a little shiver.

"I know so," he said, not allowing himself to doubt.

He helped her into her cloak, letting his hands linger a moment on her shoulders.

She turned around to him to say good-bye, and the next thing either of them knew she was in his arms and he was kissing her.

A few moments later, reluctantly, he let her go, and she squeezed his hand, then opened the front door and slipped out. What neither of them knew was that Jamie had decided to come back downstairs and had stopped in his tracks on the stairway when he saw his father kissing Alice.

That night as Rachel was helping Jamie get ready for bed, he told her what he had seen. Then he frowned at his mother. "Why was Daddy kissing her, Mom?"

Nobody, not even Rachel's severest critics, had ever said she wasn't a good mother. She was, and Jamie's politeness to adults and his generally good behavior showed it. She gave another demonstration of that good mothering now. "Are you sure he was kissing her, Jamie? Are you sure you didn't imagine it?"

"Of course I'm sure, Mom. I'm not such a baby I don't know when people kiss or don't kiss. He was kissing her."

Rachel searched for something to say. "Well, maybe it was Alice's birthday, and that's why he was kissing her." She nodded emphatically. "That's probably what it was."

"Oh," Jamie said. "I hadn't thought of that."

Rachel smiled. "You see? A perfectly simple explanation."

Jamie nodded. "And you should see Wally's new electric train, Mom. It's super."

"The next time you go there, darling, maybe I can

come along and look at it. Go brush your teeth now."

As soon as Jamie was tucked in bed, Rachel went downstairs. Once there she exchanged her role of protective mother for that of embittered wife. She called Sam at his hotel to tell him what had happened, upbraiding him for doubting her earlier when she had claimed that Steve and Alice were involved each other. "It's all right with me, Sam," she said, "if you don't want to believe me, but what reason would Jamie have to lie about something as upsetting to him as that?"

"No reason that I know of, Rachel."

"Well, are you going to do something now or not?"

"Rachel," he said with a sigh, "a kiss is not having an affair."

Even though he couldn't see it, she made an exasperated face. "Sam, I'm not stupid. I didn't say it was. But it proves the two of them are meeting, and it *practically* proves they're having one. I mean, naturally they're not going to do anything more than kiss at Lenore's house, with two children and Lenore right there. But there's nothing to stop them from doing more than that at Alice's apartment. Or Steve's either, for that matter."

Rachel took a breath, and Sam took the opportunity to say, "Are you finished, Rachel?"

By way of answer she said, "I want to know what you're going to do."

He sighed again. "There's nothing I can do. I told you once before I'm not a private eye. If you want to get yourself one, that's your privilege, but I'm staying out of it."

"You're supposed to keep Steve from getting a divorce. That's what I hired you for."

"Right. When the suit he's filed comes to a hearing, I'll be in there fighting for you."

"I want you to start fighting for me now."

"Rachel, I've already told you—"

"I know what you've already told me," she said, cutting him off. "Now I'm telling you. Either you do something about this, or I will." And she hung up on him.

Rachel didn't wait to see whether or not Sam was going to do anything. The next afternoon she drove to Lenore's house and parked in front of it until Lenore came home from Steven Frame Enterprises. As soon as Lenore drove into her driveway Rachel was out of her car and waiting in the frigid cold.

"I don't know what you think you're doing," she said as Lenore got out of her car, "but you're not going to get away with it."

A compassionate, fair-minded person, Lenore had always tried to be decent to Rachel, even when it required a great deal of effort. Drawing her coat collar about her throat, she said, "I don't know what you're talking about, Rachel, but come inside. It's too cold to stand out here."

Rachel shook her dark head. "No, I won't go inside, and you're not going to freeze in the time it takes me to say what I have to say." She hunched her shoulders against the stiff wind. "I've let Steve bring Jamie here so he could play with Wally, but I'm not going to let him do it anymore—not while you're letting Steve and Alice use your house as a meeting place."

Still clutching her coat collar, Lenore frowned. "Their meeting here yesterday was an accident, Rachel."

"Oh, sure," Rachel answered airily. "And I suppose

their kissing was an accident too."

Lenore's frown deepened. "Who said anything about kissing?"

"Jamie did. He saw Steve kissing Alice."

Lenore didn't know what to say to that—or what there was to say. All she managed was, "Oh."

Rachel seized on that. Smiling nastily, she said, "No denial, Lenore? Just 'oh'? My goodness me."

Lenore shrugged. In the chill wind it became a shiver. "I didn't see it happen, Rachel. I didn't know anything about it."

Rachel seized on that as well. "And I suppose you don't know anything about the affair they're having, either."

That, Lenore wouldn't stand still for, especially since she knew Rachel's accusation was false. "Rachel, that's a lie. Alice and Steve are not having an affair."

"That's what you say. I happen to know different."

Lenore frowned again. "From whom?"

The answer Rachel gave her was what Lenore expected. With another nasty smile she said, "I should tell you, and have you run to Alice with the information I have? No thanks, Lenore. But there is one piece of information you can run to her with, and that's this. She and Steve may think they can get away with what they're doing, but they're not going to, because I'm going to sue."

Lenore wasn't sure what Rachel was talking about, but her threatening tone was unmistakable. "Sue whom for what?" she asked.

Rachel had written the words down and practiced saying them until she could rattle them off. "I'm going to sue Alice," she said, "for alienation of affection." She turned and headed back to her car, then stopped and turned back to Lenore with another of her smiles. "Tell her to put that in her pipe and smoke it." She lifted her hand. "So long, Lenore."

Lenore watched Rachel drive off, then went into the house. Without even taking her coat off, she went to the phone in the living room and called Alice at her apartment. After telling her what Rachel had said, she added, "She's like a crazy person, Alice. I wouldn't put anything past her."

Alice didn't share her friend's alarm. "I know," she said, "but she can't file such a suit herself. She'd have to get Sam Lucas to do it for her, and John keeps telling us he's sure Sam won't do anything rash—or let *her* do anything rash, either."

"John may be right," Lenore answered, "but I wouldn't be sure of anything where Rachel is concerned. She could talk the hide off an elephant."

Alice shook her taffy-blond head. "She can talk all she wants to, Lenore, but it takes more than talk to make a lawsuit. And that's where Rachel is out of luck. Steven and I are not having an affair."

Lenore sighed. "I wish he hadn't kissed you."

"Now that I know the circumstances I wish he hadn't too. But we see each other so little and we love each other so much." Alice sighed. "Now I suppose we won't be able to see each other at all."

"I wouldn't if I were you. Not until things cool down a little. I wouldn't even talk to him on the phone. You and Steve had your phones bugged once before. It could happen again."

"I suppose that's true," Alice said, recalling the incident clearly. She sighed again. "What I really wish is that Rachel didn't have to be Rachel."

"Alice," Lenore said with a shake of her head,

"you might as well wish for the moon."

"I know. Well, thanks for calling me, Lenore, and for warning me. Let's hope nothing comes of it."

"Yes, let's." But Lenore didn't believe nothing would come of it, and she doubted Alice did either. They both knew Rachel too well.

Rachel also knew herself pretty well. She was certainly aware of the mistakes she'd made in the past, first in trying to take Steve away from Alice, and then—and now—in trying to keep Alice from taking him back.

Thinking about some of those mistakes as she drove away from Lenore's house, she pulled up to a public phone booth and called Sam at his hotel to ask if he could see her. He said he could, and she drove to the hotel.

He was at the makeshift desk working—he was always at the desk working whenever she went there to see him—but he put his work aside and turned his chair around to face her as she took her mink coat and threw it on the bed, then sat down in the armchair next to it.

"What can I do for you, Rachel?" he asked.

She looked at her carefully manicured hands. "I don't know. Maybe I just need somebody to talk to. If you have the time for me."

He frowned and searched her face. "You sound down."

"I guess I am."

"Is Jamie okay?"

"Yes, he's fine. He went to Mom's after school, and I'm going there for supper when I leave here. Then Jamie and I will go home." She lapsed into silence, clasping and unclasping her purse. At length she threw it on the bed beside her coat. "I'm not sure I ever thanked you, Sam, for getting Steve to let me have an apartment here in town."

He shook his dark head. "You're paying me, Rachel. You don't have to thank me."

"Well, still and all . . . I do thank you, Sam."

"Do you like your apartment?"

"Yes. It's very nice. And in a lovely part of town."

"Well." He spread his hands. "No more all alone out in the country."

She turned a sad face to him. "Yeah. Now it's all alone here in town." She got up from the chair and went to stare out the window at the air shaft. "It's funny how fast your life can change, isn't it?"

"Yeah, I guess so." When Rachel had telephoned asking to see him, Sam had wondered what she wanted. He wondered now if she was beginning to get to it.

She was still staring out the window, though there was nothing to see out there except a grimy brick wall about four feet away. "When Steve and I got married," she said, "I thought I was fixed for life." She half turned, as if considering what she had just said. "I shouldn't have put it that way. That makes it sound like I was talking about money, and I wasn't." She turned all the way around to look at him. "That's another funny thing, Sam—how everybody thinks I married Steve for his money, I mean. And I didn't at all."

Rachel walked to the bed and fingered her mink coat. "Oh, not that the money isn't nice, but if Steve lost every cent he had and wanted me back, I'd go like that." Letting go of the coat, she snapped her fingers, then sat down again in the easy chair. "I married him because I loved him, and because he loved Jamie and me and he wanted us to be a family. A real family." She shook her head. "I can't tell you how many times he said that to me, Sam—how he wanted us to be a family."

Still not certain what she was getting at, Sam nodded. "I'm sure he did, Rachel."

"And he didn't just say it," she went on, her voice gathering strength. "He meant it. He loves that little boy so much." She smiled, and then the smile faded away. "And we were so happy, the three of us. Steve would come home at night, and Jamie would be standing at the front window in the living room watching for him, ready to wave to him and shout, 'Daddy's home! Daddy's home!'"

Tears filled Rachel's dark eyes, and Sam held out a box of tissues to her. Taking one, she wiped her eyes, then said in a wistful voice, "I don't know why it still can't be that way for us. I swear I don't."

Maybe, Sam thought, feeling sorry for her, that was why she had come to see him—simply to pour out her misery to a willing ear. "Well, Rachel," he said, "these things happen."

She turned a pleading face to him. "They don't have to happen, Sam." Bitterness crept into her voice. "And if it hadn't been for Alice coming back to Bay City, they wouldn't be happening."

He was beginning to feel wary now, thinking there was more to Rachel's talk than just an outpouring of misery. He sought to stop her before she went too far. "Well, I'm afraid there's nothing you can do about that now, Rachel."

"Yes, there is, Sam. Or at least you could do it for me, if you only would."

Sam frowned. "Are you back to talking about alienation of affection?"

She answered his question with a question. "Isn't that exactly what she did to me?"

"Well, yeah," he admitted, "you've got a point."

Rachel leaned forward in the chair. "And is there any reason I should have to just sit back and let her do it to me? Let her get away with it?"

"Rachel—" Sam put up a hand to forestall another of her outbursts. "Now don't get your back up. I can see your side of it. I honestly can. Especially because of Jamie. But nothing has changed since we first talked about this. You can't go on hearsay. You've got to have evidence."

She settled back in her chair. "We have evidence that they've been alone together, and we have evidence that they were kissing. And we certainly have evidence that Steve has left me because of Alice."

Sam shook his head. "Now wait a minute, Rachel. You're getting carried away. We have evidence that Steve left you, period. *Why* he left you becomes your word against his."

Rachel stood up and began pacing back and forth across the floor of the little room. "Well, all right, then. Leave that part out of it. We still have the evidence of their being alone and their kissing. And we have witnesses to prove it, too."

He frowned again. "What witnesses?"

She stopped her pacing to turn to him. "Lenore, for one. One of the places they were alone was her house. And she was there at the time, so how could she say she didn't know if they were alone or not? She'd have to say she knew they were."

Sam nodded. "What other witnesses?"

"Jamie. He saw them kissing."

He stared at her, aghast. "You surely wouldn't want to bring Jamie in on a suit of this kind—pitting one parent against the other?"

Rachel hadn't taken her eyes off his face. "What do you think Steve is doing if he isn't doing that?"

"Well, I know, but Jamie isn't going to have to testify in Steve's suit. And, Rachel, even if the judge talked to Jamie privately, in chambers—and I'm sure that's how he would do it—it would still be a terrible ordeal for him."

Rachel's eyes filled with tears again, but this time she ignored the proffered tissue box, letting the tears run down her face. "Sam, don't you think what Jamie's been going through ever since his father left us has been a terrible ordeal for him?"

Sam put down the box of tissues and shook his head. "Rachel, it isn't the same."

Now Rachel resumed her pacing. "All right, it isn't the same, but who's to say one is worse than the other?" Suddenly she stopped and turned to him. "Sam, if you file this suit for me, and I win it, then there won't be any divorce—there can't be—and Steve will come back to us."

Now Sam got to his feet. "Rachel, hold on. You're jumping to all kinds of conclusions. And I want to ask you something before you jump to any more. When you asked me to be your lawyer in all this, you swore to me you had no part in what your father did to break up Steve's marriage to Alice."

She nodded. "That's right. I didn't."

"You also swore to me you didn't know about it—not until months afterward."

She nodded again. "And that's right too."

"You still swear to both?"

"Yes, of course I do." She frowned at him. "What are you getting at, Sam? Has something happened you haven't told me about?"

"No, nothing's happened."

"Well, then, what?"

Sam perched on a corner of his makeshift desk. "I'm getting to it. I've gotten to it before, but apparently it didn't stick with you. If there was no fraud on your part when you married Steve, then Steve is going to lose his suit for divorce. Do you get me?"

She nodded. "Yes."

He lifted his hands. "Well, that puts you right where you think the alienation-of-affection suit will put you—no divorce." He folded his arms across his chest. "What happens after that I'm not going to speculate about, because that's all it would be—speculation. You think Steve will come back to you. I'm just as sure he won't. But you're not paying me for what I think, so it doesn't matter."

Rachel came over to him, the pleading look again on her pretty, heart-shaped face. "Sam, what I'm paying you for is to keep Alice from taking Steve away from me, because that's what she's doing. Please file the suit for me. Please."

Sam left his perch and walked away from her, but she came after him, and the hotel room, after all, was small. She put a hand on his arm. "Please, Sam. If not for my sake, then for Jamie's. Jamie can't understand what's going on. He misses his father so much. He doesn't want to see him for a few hours one afternoon a week. He wants him home—living with us, the way he lived with us before."

Sam removed her hand from his arm. "Rachel, I just don't know. It isn't that I don't sympathize with you, but it's such a chancy thing, a suit of this kind."

She clutched at him. "Couldn't we take a chance? Oh, Sam, please. Maybe we won't win. Maybe we'll lose. But we've got to try. We've got to. I've promised Jamie I'd do everything in my power to bring his father back, and I've got to live up to that promise. Only, I can't file the suit. You've got to file it for me."

With a sigh of resignation, Sam gave in. "All right."

Rachel rewarded him with a bear hug and a beaming smile. "Oh, thank you, Sam!"

Three days later Sam came to Rachel's apartment to tell her he had changed his mind about filing the suit. He started by telling her he'd talked to Lenore, and Rachel didn't like hearing that. "What did you have to talk to her about?"

Sam took off his overcoat and laid it over the back of a chair, then sat down. "Rachel, I couldn't go into this thing feetfirst. I had to talk to her about Alice and Steve meeting at her place."

Rachel had been hovering. Now she sat down in a chair facing Sam. "Well? So?"

"She says yes, that Alice and Steve have met at her house on a number of different occasions, but she also says they have never been left alone there except the one time Jamie saw them—and that was only for a few minutes at the most."

Rachel gave him a disgusted look. "If Jamie hadn't seen what he did, Lenore wouldn't even have admitted to their being alone that one time."

Sam raised his eyebrows. "Are you saying Lenore would lie?"

Rachel shook her head wearily. "Are you saying she wouldn't? Sam, Alice is Lenore's best friend and has been practically her whole life."

"That doesn't mean she would lie under oath."

"She wasn't under oath when she was talking to you."

Rachel got up and began pacing about the room—a considerably larger and less cluttered one than Sam's hotel room. "And anyhow," she said, "even if what Lenore says is true, it's still going to make Alice and Steve look bad. I mean, what would you think if you were a judge and you heard that this man and this woman were kissing in somebody else's house while the man was trying to get a divorce from his wife? Would you think that's as far as they would go when they were really alone—in her apartment or in his?" Rachel stopped pacing and turned to fix him with a look. "Of course you wouldn't. And the judge we get isn't going to think so either."

Sam shook his head. "Rachel, you don't know anything about the law."

"Maybe not," she admitted, still standing where she'd stopped, still looking at him. "But when it comes to putting two and two together, I don't think judges are any different from anybody else." She cocked her head at him. "When are you going to file the suit, Sam?"

He shook his head again. "Rachel . . ."

She poked a finger at him. "Sam, you promised. You can't go back on a promise."

"We don't have sufficient evidence. We don't have any real evidence at all."

He might as well have saved his breath. "We have enough to make Alice look bad," Rachel retorted, "and that's the main thing. You don't know Alice the way I do, Sam. She isn't a fighter. She doesn't know how to fight for what she wants. When things go bad for Alice she runs away. And that's what she'll do this time. You wait. You'll see." Rachel permitted herself a little smile. "And that will be enough for me."

Sam resisted a little longer, but he finally gave in and

agreed once more to file the suit. On February first, a process server served Alice with a summons to answer a suit for alienation of affection that had been filed against her by Mrs. Steven Frame.

Chapter Three

Witness

Closing the door on the process server, Alice stared at the summons in disbelief, then, laughing, she walked back into the kitchen, where she and Janice were having breakfast.

Janice was making toast. Pushing the lever down, she looked at Alice and said, "What's so funny?"

Sitting back down to her bowl of cream of wheat, Alice handed the summons to Janice. "Rachel is suing me for taking Steven away from her." She shook her head. "How's that for laughs?"

"You can't be serious," Janice said, unfolding the document and looking at it. "On the other hand, I guess you can be."

Alice swallowed a mouthful of cereal and washed it down with a sip of coffee. "Lenore warned me this might happen, but I still find it hard to believe."

The toast popped up, and Alice held out a hand for one of the slices, then began buttering it. "Lenore also said Rachel was like a crazy person. *That* I don't find so hard to believe. Not anymore."

"What will you do?" Janice asked, handing the summons back to Alice.

"I don't know. Talk to John about it, I guess. See what he has to say." John was married to Alice's older sister, Pat, and one of the things Alice was grateful for was that John was Steve's lawyer. She shook her head again. "I don't know what Rachel thinks she can prove. She certainly can't prove that Steven and I are having an affair, because we're not."

Janice had buttered her slice of toast and was about to take a bite of it. "Maybe," she said before doing that, "she just wants to create a lot of talk."

Alice nodded. "I wouldn't put it past her."

After breakfast Alice called John to tell him about the summons.

"When can you come in to see me?" he asked.

"This afternoon—when I get off duty at the hospital."

"Let me check it out with Steve, Alice, and I'll get back to you."

By the time he called her she was at the hospital and halfway through her shift.

"Steve is sometimes hard to track down," John explained. "If he isn't on one project he's on another. But I finally got to him. Now, I asked him to come here at four. But I'm asking you to come at three forty-five. I want you here together to confer on this matter, but I don't want you arriving or leaving together. Do you get me?"

"Yes," Alice said. "I understand. I'll see you this afternoon, John. At three forty-five. I'll use the back stairs."

John laughed and rang off.

Alice and Steve each arrived as instructed. When they

were both seated before him at his desk, John looked from one to the other of them. "You understand, both of you," he said, "that if Rachel wins this suit it could prevent Steve from getting a divorce."

Steve frowned. "I don't see how she can win it. We haven't done anything."

Alice nodded, looking from Steve to John. "We've hardly even seen each other."

"Well, I'm sorry to say this," John said, "but from now on I don't want you to see each other at all, or talk on the phone." Seeing the anguished look they gave each other, John shook his head. "Rachel must have you under surveillance."

Steve frowned again. "What makes you say that, John?"

"How else could she have gotten evidence?"

"But I just told you. We haven't done anything for her to get evidence of."

John locked his hands behind his head. "She must have something she thinks a judge would pay attention to. Or that Sam thinks a judge would." Abruptly he removed his hands from behind his head and clasped them before him, elbows on the desk. "Sam's a good lawyer. He wouldn't file a suit like this on nothing at all. Unless . . ." His voice trailed off as a thought struck him.

Alice exchanged a look with Steve, then turned to John. "Unless what?" she prompted.

He didn't answer her, but went on pursuing whatever thought was troubling him. "Of course," he said, not looking at either of them, but staring off into space, "it's hard for me to believe Sam would do such a thing, but then Rachel is his client—and his niece as well. So I don't know."

Alice gave Steve a very worried look, and this time it was Steve who spoke. "You don't know what?" he asked. "John, would you mind letting us in on what you're thinking?"

John blinked and looked first at Steve, then at Alice. "I'm sorry," he said. "What I was thinking is that Rachel may have persuaded Sam to file this suit, not in the hope of winning it, but merely in the hope of creating a scandal. Which it could very well do."

Alice nodded. "Janice said much the same thing this morning at breakfast. And it sounds like Rachel."

"Yes," Steve agreed. "It certainly does."

"You both will be called to testify," John went on. "And Janice maybe. And more than likely Lenore, since you've met several times at her house." He shook his head. "The newspapers could easily make headlines."

"Out of what?" Alice demanded.

"Out of accusations, insinuations, whatever small admissions there might be that they could blow up into something bigger."

Steve frowned. "Such as?"

John turned to him. "Has there been any physical contact between you at all?"

"Well, yes," Steve admitted. "We've kissed a couple of times. But nothing more than that."

John shook his head again. "So you say." He put up a hand to forestall any protest. "I'm only showing you how some newspapers might react. The insinuations they might make."

"I'm beginning to see what you mean," Alice said. "But John, if Rachel has no real evidence, why would a judge even agree to hear such a suit?"

"He might not. Or *she* might not—as the case may be.

We have more and more women judges."

Alice shrugged. "Then I don't think we have anything to worry about, because Rachel *can't* have any real evidence. There simply isn't any for her to have."

With the conference concluded, Alice and Steve left at separate times, using two different exits from the office building where John had his practice. Now denied so much as the sight of Steven or the sound of his voice, Alice was no longer in a mood to laugh at Rachel's alienation-of-affection suit. The next afternoon after work, Alice stopped at Lenore's to tell her what had happened, but Steven had already filled Lenore in.

"I'm going to go see her," Lenore said, handing Alice a cup of tea before sitting down with one herself.

"Why?" Alice asked. "What good will it do?"

"It may not do any good at all," Lenore said, "but I feel responsible."

About to take a sip of her tea, Alice set the cup back in its saucer and stared at Lenore. "Lenore, that's crazy. You're in no way responsible."

Lenore shrugged. "I also think Rachel may listen to me."

Alice had no comment to that. None was needed. It was common knowledge that Rachel had been trying for years to get into Lenore's good graces, even palming herself off as one of Lenore's best friends when the occasion suited her.

But she didn't act like a best friend when Lenore went to see her. When she opened the door to Lenore she was immediately suspicious.

"May I come in, Rachel?"

"Well, yes. Come in." Rachel opened the door wider,

then closed it behind Lenore and followed her into the living room. "I don't know that I have anything to offer you."

"If you're talking about food or drink, Rachel, it's all right. I don't want anything. I just want to talk to you. May I sit down?"

"Well, yes, of course, Lenore. Sit down. My goodness," she added with a self-deprecating little laugh, "I don't know where my manners are."

When they were both seated, Lenore said, "Rachel, I've come here to ask you to drop your suit against Alice."

The small spark of friendliness that had emerged a moment before vanished. "Then you've wasted your time, Lenore, because I have no intention of dropping it."

"You can't possibly win such a suit," Lenore said.

Rachel's chin went up in a gesture of defiance. "Who says I can't?"

"You have no evidence of anything beyond one kiss."

The chin went higher. "How do you know what evidence I have or don't have?"

"Because I know there has been no wrongdoing between Alice and Steve, Rachel."

"Well, I say there has been, Lenore, and that's why I filed the suit. And anyhow, if you must know, I don't care whether I win the suit or not. All I care about is making things bad for Alice."

Lenore gave her an icy stare. "Humiliating her, you mean?"

Rachel shrugged. "If you want to call it that, call it that. The point is, when that happens, Alice will find it impossible to stay here, and so she'll leave."

"And what then, Rachel?"

"Then Steve will come back to me," Rachel said, smiling. "The same as he did before."

Everybody who knew Rachel and Alice and Steve thought Rachel had to be mad if she really believed she could get Steve back simply by humiliating Alice and driving her out of Bay City. They all tried to convince her that, whatever she did, coming back to her was the last thing Steve would do. But she refused to listen to reason.

The day after Lenore's visit, Rachel's mother, Ada, came by to see her. She sat down with Rachel in the living room, though she would have preferred the kitchen, where she felt more at home. After listening to Rachel tell her about Lenore's visit, Ada shook her head. "You're not thinking," she said. "You talk about evidence. What more evidence do you need of how Steve feels about Alice than that tape recording you have of the time they met in Eliot Carrington's suite?"

The time Ada was referring to was the reconciliation meeting between Alice and Steve. Unknown to them at the time, the suite had been bugged, and their meeting was taped. Eliot Carrington's estranged wife had given Rachel a copy of the tape. Rachel had played the tape, first for Alice and then for Steve, in her first attempt to keep him from leaving her. She had threatened to give it to a newspaper to humiliate Alice if he did leave her.

"I no longer have the tape," she told her mother now. "Steve took it away from me."

Ada shook her head. "You don't need to have it to remember what Steve said to Alice. You heard him say he loves her, he always has loved her, he never stopped loving her."

Rachel gave her mother a sulky look. "I don't see what you're getting at."

"No, of course you don't," she answered. "Because you won't let yourself see it. Because the only kind of evidence you're interested in is evidence that seems to support your side of things." Ada sighed. "What I'm getting at, Rachel, is that if you go ahead with this suit, if you do drive Alice away from Bay City, far from coming back to you, Steve is going to hate the sight of you—if he doesn't already."

Rachel shook her head. "I don't believe that."

Ada sighed again. "I didn't expect you to. There's no point in talking to you, Rachel. You've got your mind made up, and nothing is going to change it. Not reason, not sense, not anything."

Rachel stood up and began pacing. "You don't understand. It isn't possible for Steve to love Jamie the way he does—" She stopped and turned to her mother. "And you'll admit that, Mom, won't you?"

Her mother nodded. "Yes, I'll admit that. But that doesn't have anything to do with how Steve feels about you."

Rachel resumed her pacing. "It has everything to do with it. Steve can't love Jamie the way he does and not have some feeling for me. I'm Jamie's mother. Part of me is in Jamie. And Steve and I have been happy together. We *have* been."

Her mother sighed again. "'Have been' is right, Rachel. Whatever happiness you and Steve might have had you destroyed exactly the way I warned you you would—by not leaving Alice alone, by doing everything you could to make her miserable. And you're still doing it. Do you honestly think that will bring Steve back to you when that was what drove him away?" Exasperated and sad, Ada shook her head. "You don't ever seem to learn, Rachel."

But Rachel was adamant. "Mom, as long as Alice is here Steve will think he wants her. But you wait. The minute she's gone he'll come back to me. He said once before he didn't love me, that he didn't want to have anything to do with me. But when Alice left, all that changed. And it will again." Rachel came back and sat down again, a look of supreme confidence on her face. "You wait," she repeated. "You'll see."

"I don't know how you can put yourself through all this, Rachel. And for what?"

Rachel spun on her mother. "For Jamie. That's for what. When my father walked out on you, you let him go. You didn't lift a finger to stop him." Rachel's father had walked out on Ada when Rachel was a baby. Rachel had spent most of her life dreaming about her father, making up stories about him and excuses for his failure to get in touch with her, until she had finally found him in the nearby town of Somerset.

"Well," Rachel went on, "I'm not going to have Jamie brought up fatherless, the way I was because you wouldn't fight for your husband. I'm fighting for mine."

"Rachel, the only reason Steve ever became your husband is because you helped destroy his marriage to Alice."

Rachel jumped to her feet and stood glaring down at her mother. "That's not true! I had nothing to do with it."

Ada shook her head again. "I'm not talking about whether or not you helped your father trick Alice that one night. I don't believe you did have any part in that. I'm talking about all the other things you did—using Jamie to push yourself on Steve, making

Steve deceive Alice about seeing you."

"I had every right to see Steve. Steve is Jamie's father."

Ada opened her mouth to answer, then closed it. Bracing her hands against the cushion behind her, she pushed herself up out of the chair and onto her feet, forcing Rachel to step aside. She walked out to the foyer, got her coat out of the closet, and put it on.

Rachel followed her. "Where are you going?" she asked.

"Where I should have stayed," Ada said, buttoning her coat. "Home. I thought I could get you to change your mind about this suit, Rachel, but I should have known better." Ada walked to the door and opened it, then turned back with one last appeal. "Honey, please. For Jamie's sake, if nobody else's, drop the suit."

"All right," Rachel said. "Sure. I'll drop my suit if Steve will drop his. Tell him that, Mom, why don't you?"

Ada didn't answer. She just shook her head again and left.

While Ada was having her futile argument with Rachel, Steve was in John's office talking to him about both Rachel's suit and his own.

"What I'm trying to do," John told him, "is get the divorce hearing scheduled first on the calendar. I haven't been able to swing it so far, but I'm still working on it."

Ignoring John's invitation to sit, Steve had been pacing back and forth. "I feel so frustrated," he said. "So backed into a corner."

John gave him a dry look. "That's how Rachel wants you to feel—maybe in the hope you'll do something foolhardy."

Steve paced in silence a few moments. "What I'm thinking of doing," he said at last, "is flying out to San Francisco to try to track down Gerald Davis."

"How do you know he's still there?"

"I don't. But the chances are pretty good he is. I thought I'd ask at that restaurant he used to work at—before he got fired."

John shook his head. "It may be a fool's errand, Steve."

"John, it's better than sitting around here doing nothing. And we need Davis's testimony. You've felt all along we have a weak case."

"I didn't say weak," John corrected him. "I said uncorroborated. Of course it would be better if we had Davis to testify in your behalf. But even without him, we won't have any trouble establishing all the lies Rachel has told in the past in order to get what she wanted."

Steve went back to his pacing. "I want the case airtight. I don't want to risk losing it."

"And what if you find Gerald Davis and he won't back you up?"

Steve stopped and frowned at John. "Why wouldn't he back me up?"

John shrugged. "Any number of reasons. For one thing, he's Rachel's father. For another, it was because of his conniving—or partly, anyhow—that you ended up marrying Rachel. If he wanted to see her married to you in the first place, why wouldn't he want to see her continue to be married to you?"

"I'm not interested in what he wants," Steve said harshly. "I'm interested in what he knows."

John shrugged again. "You may never be certain of what he knows. If he wants to protect Rachel—and there's no reason to assume he doesn't—then he might lie the same as she does. That may be where she picked up her facility for lying in the first place."

Steve walked to the chair where he'd set his briefcase. "I'd like to judge for myself whether Gerald Davis is lying or not," he said. He picked up the briefcase. "You've made up my mind for me, John. I'm going out to San Francisco to track him down."

John shook his head. "I wish you wouldn't."

"Why?"

"Because you're too impulsive, Steve. And you take too many shortcuts when you're determined to get your own way. Now, that may be all right in a business deal, but it can raise all sorts of problems when it comes to the law. Let me put somebody on to finding him."

For a moment Steve considered. Then he made a decision he would later profoundly regret. "Let me have a crack at it first. If I can't find him, then we'll hire somebody."

John sighed. "I guess if your mind is made up, there's nothing I can do to stop you."

Steve nodded. "That's right. There isn't."

John got up from his desk to see Steve out. He gave him an anxious look. "You will be careful though?"

"Yes. I'll be careful."

"And you won't do anything unethical?"

Steve held up his right hand as if he were taking an oath. "Scout's honor, old friend."

John sighed again. "All right. But I still don't like it."

Steve put a hand on John's arm. "If I find Gerald and nail him down, I guarantee you'll like it then. Because I'm convinced Gerald knows the truth and will tell it to me—and, more important, to the court. And once that happens I'll be free of Rachel for good."

John held the door for Steve, then stood there looking after him as he walked through the outer office and out into the corridor. Then he closed his door and went back to his desk, telling himself everything would be all right. But he didn't believe that, and he wished he'd been able to persuade Steve not to go to San Francisco. He still didn't like the idea. Not a bit.

Steve had no trouble locating Gerald Davis once he got to San Francisco. Rachel's father was working in a fast-food hamburger shop. And he agreed readily enough to see Steve in his room at the Mark Hopkins Hotel when he got off work at the end of the afternoon. He arrived when he said he would, but he didn't look the least bit pleased about being there. Still dressed in his counterman's clothes, a five o'clock shadow on his face, looking as paunchy around the middle as he had in Bay City, Gerald was in a hostile, suspicious frame of mind.

Steve supposed he couldn't blame him. The last time they met, Gerald had asked Steve to set him up in the restaurant business, and Steve had turned him down in no uncertain terms.

He said now in a surly way, "I can't believe you came all the way out here just to see me, Steve."

"Well, I did," Steve answered, trying to sound hospitable. "What can I get you to drink?"

Steve had ordered a bottle of scotch from room service, and Gerald eyed it on the dresser. He shrugged. "Scotch and water's okay."

Steve fixed scotch and water for both of them, taking ice cubes from the silver bucket on the tray. He handed Gerald his drink.

Gerald toasted him—more or less—then said, "What can I do for you?"

Steve returned the toast. "I have a favor to ask of you."

Gerald took a swallow of his drink. "That figures. Sure. You're looking for a job, and you thought I might help you get one."

That figured, too, Steve thought, as the two men took chairs facing one another. "I'm sorry I wasn't able to help you that time, Gerald," he said, and took a swallow of his own drink.

Gerald waved a hand. "Oh, yeah. Sure. What favor are you looking for out of me, Steve—old buddy?"

Steve decided he might as well get to the point. "I want you to testify at a divorce hearing. I've filed suit for a divorce from Rachel."

"No kidding." The surly look was replaced by one of interest.

Steve's hopes rose. "That's right."

Gerald took another swallow of his drink, buying time to think over his response. "What does Rachel have to say about that?"

"She's contesting it. That's why I need your help."

Gerald frowned. "I don't know what help I could be to you—even assuming I wanted to."

"You could do what I said, testify for me."

"Testify to what?"

"That Rachel was in collusion with you when you arranged to have Alice meet me at my office the night she left me."

Gerald shook his dark head. "I already told you she wasn't. I told you that months ago. It was all my doing. Rachel didn't know anything about it."

Steve stared at him. "I don't believe you."

"You can believe what you want to. I'm telling you the truth. Rachel didn't have any part in it. None."

Gerald smiled maliciously. "Looks like you had yourself a trip for nothing."

Steve was still staring at him in disbelief. "Rachel didn't have any part in it? Not any at all?"

Gerald shook his head again. "No. None. Oh, she wanted to marry you, I don't deny that, and she did what she could to find ways to be with you. She even used Jamie to find ways to be with you. But you'll never get her to admit to that, and if anybody else accuses her of it, she'll deny doing it. You know Rachel."

"Yes," Steve said. "Only too well." He was bitterly disappointed. So much so that when Gerald finished his drink, Steve wanted nothing more than for him to go and leave him to his misery. But instead he got up to fix Gerald another drink.

Gerald accepted the refill with another of his malicious smiles. "You and Rachel couldn't make a go of it?"

Steve returned to his chair. "No."

"That's a real shame."

Curbing the temptation to light into him, Steve said, "What's really a shame, Gerald, is what you did to me that night you tricked Alice into coming to my office."

Gerald had the grace to look uncomfortable, but all he said was, "Yeah . . . well."

Steve eyed him coldly. "You could undo it."

"I don't see how."

Steve remembered what John had said to him, and hesitated. Then he pushed the warning out of his mind. He'd be damned if he was going to stay married to Rachel. "You could testify that Rachel was in collusion with you."

For some time Gerald was silent. Finally he said, "That would be lying. Lying under oath. A man can get in big trouble lying under oath."

Steve didn't take his eyes from Gerald's face. "Not if the man sticks to his story the way I intend to stick to mine."

Gerald looked interested again. "Yeah? And what's your story?"

Steve shrugged. "That I flew out here, looked you up, asked you to testify to what I believed to be the truth, and you agreed to." Steve finished his drink. "Reluctantly, of course. A man doesn't like testifying against his daughter, particularly when she's a daughter he's very fond of. But in the interest of truth and in the interest of righting a wrong, et cetera, et cetera."

"I see." Gerald used his finger to stir the ice cubes in his drink. "And what's in it for me—other than in the interest of truth and righting a wrong, et cetera, et cetera."

Once again Steve pushed the memory of John's warning out of his mind. "Ten thousand dollars."

The malicious smile turned sly. "For a reluctant father? A man who doesn't like testifying against his daughter, particularly seeing as how fond I am of Rachel?"

Steve could almost feel sorry for Rachel, to have such a father as this, but he curbed the temptation. It wasn't his fault that Gerald Davis was her father. "Fifteen thousand."

Gerald positively beamed. "Steve, you just got yourself a witness."

Chapter Four
False Hope

Beyond the kiss between Alice and Steve that Jamie had observed, the only real evidence Rachel had that Steve and Alice might be having an affair was the tape of their reconciliation that day in Eliot Carrington's hotel suite. Indeed, what was recorded on that tape was far better than a single kiss. There were all those protestations of love, and the pauses that had to be kisses, and Steve saying he would get free of Rachel, however he had to do it. That was the kind of evidence Rachel needed.

And there was the further consideration that Rachel didn't want to put Jamie through the ordeal of telling what he had seen to a judge, even in the judge's chambers.

She had to get her tape back.

Before Rachel and Steve were married, when he was still living in the bachelor apartment atop his office, Steve had given Rachel a key to the apartment and to the private elevator that led to it. After they were married and living in the house out in the country, the bachelor apartment once again became housing for visiting out-of-town staff, or a retreat for Steve when he wanted to work alone and undisturbed. He had asked Rachel to return her two keys to him, but she kept finding one excuse after another not to, claiming finally that she had lost them.

He had talked about having the locks changed, and she supposed he had, but on the off chance he hadn't, she went to his office building while he was out of town on a business trip—he was, in fact, in San Francisco, but she didn't know that. She went at night, when there would be only the night security man to stop her, figuring surely he wouldn't dare do that when she had the keys to both the elevator and the apartment. Assuming the keys still worked.

To her surprise and delight they did. Nor did the night security man try to stop her. He barely glanced at her.

The apartment was in darkness, but she fumbled around in the foyer until she found the light switch. The living room lights were on a dimmer system and were connected to Steve's stereo as well, so as the living room took shape in the soft, shadowy light, soft music began to play. The apartment was all leather and chrome, a man's apartment, and for a few minutes Rachel simply stood in the foyer drinking it all in. And with it came the memories: of the night she had first seduced Steve here, the night their son Jamie had been conceived, and then of the nights a long time after that, when Steve had been deserted by Alice and had once again turned to Rachel. As he would a third time, after she had driven Alice away again.

Coming to, remembering her purpose in visiting here, and aware that the night security man might also eventually remember that he'd been told she was not to be allowed up here, Rachel put her memories behind her and began searching for the tape recording.

Steve had dozens of tapes, most of them music, some of them business conferences of one kind or another, none of them the one she was looking for.

After searching for nearly three hours, listening to the beginning of tape after tape, she had nothing. Angry, frustrated, she slammed out of the apartment, barely remembering to turn off the switch that controlled the light and music. Not until she was in her car, driving back to her own apartment, did a solution occur to her. She slapped a hand against the wheel, wondering why she hadn't thought of it sooner. She would go to Eliot Carrington and ask him to make her another copy of the tape.

She called him the next morning, saying she had to see him, it was urgent, it would take up hardly any of his time. He sounded puzzled, but he finally said she could stop by at noon.

When he opened the door of his suite to her, she thought—and not for the first time—that Iris Carrington had to be crazy to have left this man. He was tall and lean, with a long lean face somewhat like Rachel's handsome first husband, Russ Matthews. But Eliot wasn't dark like Russ. His hair was a lighter brown. Nor was his smile as sweet.

Still, she thought as he greeted her and ushered her into the living room of the suite, she wouldn't have said no to any invitation he might make to her.

The only invitation he made to her now was to sit down. As she did so, he said, "What can I do for you, Rachel?"

She flashed him her most winning smile. "Help me, I hope."

He gave her a puzzled look. "In what way?"

Rachel knew that Eliot Carrington would be on Alice's side in this matter. She still believed that he and Alice had once had an affair, even though nobody else except Iris Carrington believed it. Still, she had learned a few things in her association with Sam Lucas, one of them being that if you wanted something from somebody, and the somebody didn't want to give it to you, you could subpoena them for it.

Rachel smiled at him again. "Do you remember the tape recording Iris made of the time Steve and Alice met here in your suite?"

He nodded. "Yes."

"And she gave me a copy."

He nodded again. "Yes, I know she did."

"Well, I no longer have it, so I need another copy of it."

He frowned. "And that's what you came here for?"

She could tell from his expression of disgust that he was not going to give her a copy voluntarily. "Yes," she said, answering his question. "That's what I came here for. Of course I realize how you feel about Alice, and that you might not want to give me one, but I can still go to court and—"

He held up a hand to cut her off. "If I'd known what you wanted, Rachel, I could have saved you the trip. All of the tapes that Iris made—and all of the transcripts that were made from the tapes—have been destroyed."

Rachel stared at him wide-eyed. "All of them?"

"All of them. I burned the lot months ago."

She was still staring at him. "Even including the one that—"

He cut her off again. "Including that one, yes. I burned them all. I'm sorry," he added, not sounding sorry at all. "Now if that's all you came here for . . ."

Rachel knew an invitation to leave when she heard one. She stood up. "Yes, that's all I came here for."

And she left.

Her meeting with Eliot Carrington was a hard surprise for Rachel. It had never occurred to her that he would have destroyed all the tapes. But she had a still harder surprise two days later, when Sam came to her apartment to see her.

"What's up?" she asked, ushering him into her living room.

"Bad news," he said, slipping out of his coat and throwing it over the arm of the chair he sat in. "The judge dismissed your suit."

About to sit down herself, Rachel turned to stare at him. "What do you mean he dismissed it?"

Sam shrugged. "Just what I said."

"But, Sam, we haven't had the hearing yet."

"That's what I'm trying to tell you, Rachel. There isn't going to be a hearing."

"But there has to be."

Sam shook his head. "Not if the judge rules otherwise. And that's what he did."

"But why?"

"For lack of evidence. I told you in the beginning you had to have evidence, and you didn't have any."

Rachel stood in front of her chair, clenching and unclenching her hands. "You didn't tell me there wouldn't even be a hearing on it."

"I thought that was obvious."

"Well, it wasn't. At least with a hearing it would have

made the papers. Now nobody will know a thing about it."

Sam shook his head again. "I'm sorry."

"You're sorry," she sneered at him. "A lot you care. A lot anybody does. This whole city is on the side of the Matthewses. It always has been."

Sam said nothing. There was nothing to say to that kind of remark that wouldn't make her angrier than she already was.

"Well, I'll show them," she said, beginning to pace back and forth across the room. "I will, I will. Only, I can't do it alone."

Beginning to feel uncomfortable at continuing to sit while Rachel was on her feet, Sam stood up and leaned against a highboy that stood on the side wall of the room. "You're not alone, Rachel," he said as soothingly as he could. "You've got me. You've got your mother."

"Oh, yes," she said with a shake of her dark head. "For all the good that does me. Mom has always sided with the Matthews family. Always. Even before I married Russ. And you—" she made a scornful face— "you're thick as thieves with John Randolph. I should have known you'd do everything you could to protect Alice and her friends—to keep them from having to get up in court to answer my accusations."

Sam was getting a bit hot under the collar himself now. "Rachel," he said, stepping away from the highboy, "that's not true."

She stopped her pacing to confront him. "Well, that's how it turned out, isn't it?"

"Yes, and I've already told you why. Because you had no evidence to back up your accusations. That's why the judge threw the case out of court."

"So you say."

Sam turned to pick up his coat. "Okay, Rachel," he said. "That does it. Get yourself another lawyer. I'm bowing out," and he headed for the door to her apartment.

"Sam," she cried out, running after him, "you can't do that!"

Already at the door, he turned to face her. "Who says I can't?" He could barely control his anger.

She began to cry. "Sam, you can't walk out on me. I don't know any other lawyers. I'm sorry I said what I did. I didn't mean it. I was upset, that's all." She clasped her hands together beseechingly. "Sam, please. I haven't had an easy day or night since Steve walked out on me. Sam, you've got to help me. Please."

He stood there a moment looking at her. Finally, with a sigh, he said, "All right, Rachel. But no more fireworks. Is that agreed?"

"Yes," she said. "That's agreed."

He looked at his watch. "And as long as I'm halfway out the door, why don't I go on back to the hotel now anyhow? It's the end of a long day for me, and I'm tired. You probably are too. We can get together tomorrow, when we're fresher."

"No!" she cried out, then turned a frightened face to him. "I mean, I didn't mean it to sound like I'm defying you, but—Sam, I can't let Steve win the divorce hearing. If he does, then it's all over for me."

Sam hadn't moved from the door, and he didn't move now. "Rachel," he said as gently as he could, "I don't want to build false hopes—I certainly don't want to do that. But I don't see how he can win it. Not when the burden of proof is on his side, and he has only his word against yours."

She nodded. "That's why I want you to come back in

and sit down with me. Because I want it to be more than that." She turned and walked back into the living room and sat down on the sofa. With a shrug and another sigh he followed her, sitting beside her. He supposed she was thinking about her father, and he was right.

"I want you to go to San Francisco and talk to my father. Get him to come back with you and testify for me. Then we'll know for sure that Steve can't win."

Sam frowned. "I don't have to go to San Francisco to talk to him. I can talk to him from here." His frown deepened. "But I thought you were on the outs with your father."

She nodded again. "Well, I was, but that was way back last fall. He won't still be holding that against me. And anyhow, it wasn't my fault Steve wouldn't set him up in business. I did what I could to help him. I made an appointment for him with Steve."

Becoming agitated again, Rachel got to her feet and began pacing. "Oh, why did you have to bring all that up again? If it hadn't been for my father telling Steve how he'd tricked Alice—telling him just so he could get back at Steve for turning him down—Steve and I would still be living together, and Alice wouldn't even be here."

"Rachel," Sam protested, "I didn't bring it up. You did." With a resigned sigh, he suggested, "Maybe we should leave your father out of this."

Rachel came back and sat down beside him. "No. It's the least he can do for me after all the damage he did. But you'll have to talk to him, Sam, because every time I think of what he did, I—"

"All right, Rachel," Sam cut in, not wanting another emotional outburst, "I'll talk to him. You get me his phone number, and I'll call him. You understand we'll have to pay his travel expenses?"

Rachel went to a small, cluttered desk next to the highboy. "I don't care what we have to pay. Just get him here." She began riffling through the papers on the desk. "I've got his number here somewhere. Or at least I think I do."

Sam stood up and walked over to the desk. "Do you want me to call him now?"

"Why not?" She was still riffling through papers, opening drawers and shutting them. Finally she pounced on a scrap of paper. "Here. Here it is. I knew it was in here somewhere." She handed the scrap paper to Sam.

He took it with him to the phone, dialed the number, and waited. "It's ringing," he said. Then, into the phone, "Hello, Mr. Davis? Gerald? This is Sam Lucas, Ada's brother . . . Yeah, that's right. . . . No, I'm not calling for her. I'm calling for Rachel. About her divorce hearing. Or I guess I should say Steve's divorce hearing, since he's the one who's suing her . . . Yeah, yeah, that's right . . . Well, he walked out on her last summer, and now he wants a divorce. And Rachel is contesting it . . . Well, because she doesn't want it. And she needs your help; that's why I'm calling."

While Sam talked to her father, Rachel perched on the edge of the sofa, trying to figure out what her father was saying by listening intently to Sam's end of the conversation. Finally Sam put a hand over the mouthpiece and turned to her. "I'm getting nowhere."

Before Rachel could say anything Sam was speaking into the phone again. "But I just explained that, Gerald. It's all right if I call you Gerald, isn't it? . . . Well, yeah, that too. Look. Hold on a minute, will you?" Again he put a hand over the mouthpiece, and said, "I'm still getting nowhere."

She frowned at Sam. "Why not?"

Sam shrugged. "First he said he didn't know anything about it, and then when I explained it to him, he started making excuses: He hasn't been feeling up to par. He's busy. The man he works for doesn't like his employees to take time off. It's a long way to come." He shrugged again. "You name it, he'll come up with it."

Rachel's frown deepened. "But he's got to come."

"Then you'd better get on the phone to him yourself." He motioned to her to take the instrument, his hand still over the mouthpiece. "Just be careful what you say, that's all. I mean, you're the one who has something to lose in this, Rachel. It's no skin off your father's nose whether you stay married to Steve or not. Right?"

"Yes," she said. "Right."

Rachel got up to take the phone from him, but for a moment he held it back. "Then watch what you say to him. Okay? Don't start accusing him, anything like that. That's just going to turn him off."

Rachel was beginning to get impatient. "All right, Sam. All right. I know what not to say to him. Give me the phone." He held it out to her, and she took it. "Daddy?" she said into it, her voice soft. "It's Rachel."

"Yeah," her father said. "I recognize your voice. How are you, Rachel?"

"Daddy, I'm desperate. I need your help so badly."

"Yeah, well . . ."

"Please don't say no. Please say you'll come to Bay City and testify for me."

"Rachel, I told Sam I—"

She cut him off, but she was careful not to raise her voice. "Yes, I know what you told him. I know it's a lot

I'm asking of you. But I have to ask it, Daddy. I can't let Steve divorce me. I can't bring Jamie up the way I was brought up—without a father to help me."

"Rachel, honey, I appreciate what you're going through, but—"

"Daddy, please. If you'll only help me this one time I won't ever ask it again. I promise. Daddy, please say you'll come. I beg of you. Please."

There was a moment or two of silence, and then her father sighed, a long, long sigh. "All right, Rachel. I'll be there."

"Oh, Daddy," she said, beaming into the phone. "And you'll back me up? You'll testify that I didn't know anything about what you did that night?"

There was another moment of silence, and then all he said was, "I'll be there, Rachel. I'll be there."

"Oh, Daddy, thank you. Thank you so much. I look forward so much to seeing you. Oh, Daddy, I love you so!"

"Good-bye, Rachel," he said.

"Good-bye, Daddy," Rachel cradled the phone, then gave Sam a big hug. "Oh, I knew I could talk him into coming here. I knew I could. Oh, Sam, we're going to win this case! There's no way we can lose it now! Oh, thank heaven for my father!"

"You said it," Sam said, grinning. "Well, I've thought all along we would win, but this is the clincher."

While Rachel was crowing over her anticipated victory, Steve Frame was sitting in John's office reporting on the success of his trip to San Francisco.

"I must confess," John said, settling back in his swivel chair, tapping a pencil against the fingers of his hand, "I don't understand Gerald Davis's willingness to testify in your behalf. Especially after the way you threw him out of your office the last time he was here."

Steve kept his face buried in his briefcase, checking some papers there. "Maybe he has a short memory," he said.

It wasn't the best response he could have made. John frowned and said, "He'd better not have if his testimony is going to amount to anything." His frown deepened. "Steve, are you sure you didn't smooth the way for him? Expense money plus something on the side?"

"No," Steve said. "Nothing."

John shook his head. "Then I don't understand it at all. Why should he risk losing Rachel's affection to give testimony for somebody he has no feeling for at all? Or if he does have, it's a grudge."

Steve wished this meeting over and tried to come up with the most reasonable reply he could think of. "John," he said, "can't you grant Gerald Davis any conscience at all?"

"Not very easily."

"Well, easily or not easily, he knows what he did was wrong. And it's not just me he's doing it for. He's doing it for Alice. Probably more for Alice than for me." Steve got to his feet. "The main thing is he agreed to do it. Let him worry about Rachel and how she'll take it." He looked at his watch. "And now I've really got to get on out of here. That trip put me behind schedule on a couple of projects."

John stood up with him. "Okay, Steve. I'll see you at the hearing, then."

Steve nodded. "Yeah. Day after tomorrow. Bright and early. See you, John."

And Steve left before John could voice any more of

the doubts that still clouded his face. Steve felt guilty, but only a little. He still believed Rachel had been in collusion with her father. Gerald was lying, that was all. So, tit for tat.

Sam's alarm clock had just gone off, and he was getting out of bed, yawning, when the phone in his hotel room rang. Picking it up, he said, "Yeah? Hello."

"Sam?" It was Rachel. "Have you heard from my father?"

"No." He thought to himself that that must mean she hadn't heard from him either. And this was the morning of the hearing. "But I didn't expect to hear from him, Rachel. You're the one I'd expect him to call."

"Well," Rachel said, sounding apprehensive, "I haven't heard a word from him. You don't suppose he's changed his mind about coming, do you?"

Sam yawned again. "I don't know. Maybe he flew in last night, and it was too late to get in touch with you." He peered at his travel alarm. "It's only a little after seven, Rachel. That's only four o'clock San Francisco time. And the hearing's been put off until two o'clock this afternoon."

Rachel was beginning to sound belligerent. "How would my father know that?"

Sam shook his head. "With an illegal casino operation in his background, your father can't be a stranger to court procedures and postponements. Maybe he called the court yesterday afternoon to check it out."

"Maybe," she agreed reluctantly.

He yawned a third time. "Give your father a couple more hours anyhow."

"All right." Rachel sighed. "I wish this whole business

was over. I hardly slept at all last night."

"You can catch up on your sleep tonight."

She turned grumpy. "I don't know what you have to sound so cheerful about."

It was hard under ordinary circumstances for Sam to keep up with Rachel's lightning changes in mood. It was doubly hard when he was only barely awake. "Relax, Rachel. We're going to win this case."

"Are we?" She sounded doubtful.

Sam frowned into the mouthpiece. "Of course we are. We've got the truth on our side. And we've got your father on our side to back us up."

"If he comes, we've got him."

"He said he'd be here, didn't he?"

"Yes, but that doesn't mean he will. My father isn't the most reliable person you'd ever want to meet. We both know that."

Sam shook his head—and yawned again. "Relax, Rachel. I'm sure he'll be here. If he weren't coming you would have heard something before now."

"I hadn't thought of that," Rachel said, and now she sounded relieved. "I guess you're right, Sam. I'll see you later."

While Sam was showering and getting dressed, Rachel was checking the town's hotels and motels to see if her father was registered anywhere. He wasn't. She then tried calling him in San Francisco. There was no answer.

Checking the phone book, she called a couple of other motels a little distance out of Bay City. No luck. Then she remembered that the time her father had come to ask Steve to set him up in business, he had said he was staying in town. With some friend probably. She had been so relieved not to have to put him up at the house, she hadn't asked who his friend was, so there was no way of checking that out. But that was probably where he was.

With a sigh, she put the phone book away, wondering why her father hadn't called her, persuading herself finally that he had probably tried to do but hadn't been able to reach her because her own line was busy with all the calls she'd been making. Or maybe he wanted to be able to say to the judge that he had not conferred with his daughter about his testimony beyond telling her on the phone a few days ago that he would come to Bay City to testify.

Satisfied with that, Rachel showered and dressed, putting on a lime green wool flannel suit with a yellow silk blouse—an outfit that made her look her prettiest and her most demure. Earlier court appearances had proved to her that the injured party was best off looking demure and vulnerable.

When she arrived in the lounge at the courthouse where she was to meet Sam, it was a full ten minutes before two, but Sam was there ahead of her. Getting to his feet, he beamed at her. "That's a great outfit, Rachel. Perfect."

She pirouetted for him. "I'm glad you like it, Sam."

"Did you hear from your father?"

"No," she answered, then repeated for him all her speculations on why he hadn't called.

Sam shrugged. "Any one of those might be the case, I guess." He checked his watch. "Well, we'd better go on into the courtroom. We don't want to be late."

"No," she agreed, and together they set off.

Rachel was surprised—though she told herself she shouldn't have been—to see all the Matthews family there: Jim and Mary and John's wife, Pat. Even Russ was there, though he had to have taken time off from the hospital to do it. And Alice was there, of course, wearing a blue dress and looking vulnerable too. But then, except when she was laughing, Alice always looked vulnerable. It was natural to her.

And of course Steve was there, sitting at the plaintiff's table talking to John Randolph. As Rachel and Sam sat down at the defense table, John smiled at Sam, but Steve didn't even look up.

The courthouse clock was striking two when the clerk of the court announced the judge. Everybody stood up until the judge came in, took his place, and rapped his gavel, and the clerk instructed them to be seated.

The clerk then stood in front of the bench and read from a paper announcing the suit. When he had finished that, he called as the plaintiff's first witness the nurse who had taken Gerald Davis's call at the hospital.

John stood up. "Your honor," he said, "since drawing up the list of the plaintiff's prospective witnesses for the benefit of the court and the defense, we have added a further witness—a surprise witness—that we would like to call now to the stand."

The judge turned to Sam. "Do you have any objection?"

Sam shook his head. "No, sir. I have no objection." Turning to Rachel, he said in a low voice, "Do you know anything about this?"

"No," she said, shaking her head.

"I wonder who it could be."

Hearing a stir at the rear of the courtroom, Rachel turned to see who was coming in. It was her father. She stared at him, her face going white. Then she gasped and said, "I don't believe it. I don't believe it."

She had spoken in a low voice to Sam, but in the hush that had fallen over the spectators at the sight of Rachel's father, everybody in the room heard what she said.

Chapter Five
Love Trap

The hush continued in the courtroom as Gerald Davis made his way down the aisle. Rachel was still staring at her father in wide-eyed disbelief, her face still drained of color. He didn't look at her. Even when he took his place in the witness box, and she came into his line of vision, he still didn't look at her. He focused his attention on John Randolph, who stepped to the box to question him, or else he looked down at his hands, clenched together in his lap.

After establishing his identity, the dates he lived in Bay City and why he had lived there, John said, "As a part owner and subsequent manager of the Hearthside Inn, were you on the premises of that restaurant a substantial portion of the time?"

Gerald gave a curt nod. "I was there ten to twelve hours a day, seven days a week."

"Was your daughter, Rachel, often there with you?"

"Yeah—yes. She worked there pretty long hours herself."

"And when Rachel's husband at that time—Ted

Clark—when Ted Clark returned home from serving a term in prison, was he often at the restaurant?"

Gerald nodded again. "Yes. Rachel had been standing in for him while he was gone, and when he came back he took over from her."

"Meaning she no longer worked there?"

"Not on a regular basis, no. But sometimes she helped out if we were shorthanded."

John looked at his notes, then back at Gerald. "So you continued to see Rachel?"

"Well, sure," Gerald answered, sounding belligerent. "I saw her a lot, whether she was working there or not."

At the defense table Sam got to his feet. "Your Honor, I don't see what all this—"

John cut him off. "He will see, Your Honor, with my next question."

The judge nodded. "Very well. Get to it."

Sam sat back down.

"Mr. Davis," John said, "did you have the opportunity to observe the quality of the relations between your daughter, Rachel, and her husband, Ted Clark?"

"Yes, I did. And I can save you the next question. They weren't getting along at all. They quarreled and bickered, that sort of thing."

John frowned. "Both of them? Equally?"

Gerald frowned too. "Well, no. I wouldn't say that. Once they got started quarreling, they both went at it, but Ted wanted the marriage to work. Rachel didn't."

Rachel hadn't taken her eyes off her father since his appearance in the courtroom, and she didn't now.

"How do you know that?" John was saying.

Gerald spread the hands he had been clenching. "She

told me so. Rachel used to talk to me a lot about her personal affairs. She confided in me."

"I see," John said. He looked at his notes again. "Can you tell me exactly when Rachel decided she didn't want her marriage to Ted Clark to continue?"

"Not exactly, no. But it was around the time he got out of prison. Maybe before that. Rachel came to the conclusion that Ted Clark was a loser, and I agreed with her. I thought he was too."

At the defense table Rachel took her eyes off her father long enough to turn to Sam and whisper, "He's telling it backwards. He was the one who kept telling me what a loser Ted was—until I finally agreed with him."

Sam made a note, but he whispered back to her, "I don't know that it makes much difference, Rachel. But we'll see."

Rachel turned back to the witness stand. John was saying to her father, "When Rachel concluded that her husband was—as you put it—a loser, did she say anything to you about what action she intended to take, if any?"

"Yes," Gerald said, nodding. "She intended to divorce Ted and marry Steve Frame."

John gave him a puzzled look. "But Steve Frame was married at the time to Alice Matthews Frame."

Gerald nodded again. "I know that. She intended to do something about that, too."

At the defense table Rachel muttered. "That's not true," but she said it only to herself—and didn't herself believe it.

"What could she do?" John asked.

"Well," Gerald answered, "she had her son, Jamie—their son, Jamie, hers and Steve's."

Now John gave the witness a surprised look. "Are you telling me that your daughter, Rachel, had been previously married to Steve Frame?"

Gerald shook his head. "No. She was married to Russ Matthews when she had Jamie. But the kid was Steve Frame's. Everybody knew that, and nobody denied it. Not even Steve himself."

At the plaintiff's table Steve sat looking down at his hands, but out in the courtroom Jim and Mary Matthews exchanged glances, and Russ and Alice did too.

Standing at the witness stand, John nodded. "I see. All right. To get back to Rachel's son, Jamie—her son by Steven Frame. How did Rachel expect to use Jamie to break up Steve's marriage to Alice?"

Before Gerald could answer, Rachel was on her feet shouting, "That's not true! I didn't do any such thing!"

The judge gave her a sour look. "Young woman," he began.

Sam pulled Rachel down onto her chair. "Be quiet," he said in a low voice, "or you'll get thrown out of here."

"I don't care," she snapped at him. "It's not true."

He had a firm grip on her hand, and he kept it. "Rachel, we'll get our chance later. Just hold your horses. And say what you have to say to me." He looked up at the judge. "Sorry, Your Honor."

The judge looked at him. "I won't have any more such outbursts."

"No, sir," Sam said.

In the spectators' section the various members of the Matthews family exchanged glances again. Rachel's mother, Ada, sat a little away from them. She sighed, a sad look on her worn face.

John went back to his questioning. "Let me repeat

what I asked you. How did Rachel expect to use Jamie to break up Steve's marriage to Alice?"

Rachel shifted in her chair, and Sam put a warning finger on her wrist.

Gerald spread his hands again. "She was always thinking up ways to get to meet Steve, to talk to him about Jamie."

Again John put on a look of surprise. "Wouldn't it be natural for a mother to want to confer with her son's father about matters concerning their son?"

"You bet it would be," Rachel muttered, and Sam gave her a warning glance.

Gerald answered the question with a long statement. "The two couples—Rachel and Ted and Steve and Alice—had an agreement, a written agreement, about Steve's seeing Jamie: when he would see him, and where, and all that. Rachel wasn't part of the deal. She was supposed to stay strictly away from Steve—not have any contact with him at all. On account of what had happened in the past. Between them. You know."

John nodded. "I see."

"But," he went on, "Rachel was always finding ways to get around that. Like the last time she did it. She hadn't let Steve see Jamie at all for—oh, I don't know how long. Long enough to make Steve mad, at any rate."

John put on another look of surprise. "But I thought you said there was an agreement about Steve's seeing Jamie."

"There was. But Rachel decided she'd had enough of that agreement. It didn't suit her anymore. So she just plain refused to let Steve see Jamie."

Out in the spectators' section Ada sighed again. She had known for a long time that sooner or later Rachel's transgressions would come back to haunt her. Whatever reason Gerald had for testifying on Steve's side of this case, he had so far spoken the truth.

"And there was no way Steve could get at him," Gerald was saying. "He couldn't even get Rachel on the phone. If she was there when he called, she pretended not to be, and she wouldn't respond to any of the messages he left."

Once again Rachel shifted in her chair, and again Sam put a warning finger on her wrist.

John checked his notes. "And you say this was all part of a scheme Rachel had to get to see Steve herself?"

"That's right," Gerald said, nodding. "And it was part of a bigger scheme than that. Rachel came to me and asked me to help her trap Steve into a situation that would break up his marriage to Alice."

Rachel shot up from the defense table, and this time she didn't shout her protest, she screamed it. "That's not true! He's lying! It was all his doing. His alone. I had no part in it! None!"

Sam was on his feet trying to shut her up, but she burst into tears, sobbing, "My father's lying. He's lying!"

"Rachel," Sam said, "please."

He couldn't stem the flow of tears. Or words. "He's lying," Rachel repeated, sobbing. "My father's lying."

In the courtroom, Alice and Russ exchanged a meaningful glance. They had both had long experience with Rachel's lies and sobbing protests. Jim and Mary Matthews also exchanged glances, and their older daughter, Pat, John Randolph's wife, seated next to her mother, squeezed Mary's hand. For her part, Rachel's mother, Ada, suffered in lonely silence.

After a long look at the still-sobbing Rachel, the

judge tapped his gavel and said, "Court will be in recess for fifteen minutes."

"All rise," the bailiff said, and all did so as the judge left the room. Then the courtroom cleared.

Rachel didn't want to leave. She wanted to stay where she was, but Sam said, "Look, Rachel, when court reconvenes the judge will expect you to have your emotions back under control, and if you just sit here for the next fifteen minutes feeling sorry for yourself, that isn't going to happen. Now come on out in the hall with me. You can get yourself a drink of water, go to the ladies' room—whatever."

So she went.

Out in the hall the various spectators stood in little huddles, talking in low tones. Gerald Davis was nowhere to be seen.

After looking around for him, Rachel went over to her mother. "Mom," she said, "he's lying."

"Yes," Ada said, "I know he is."

Through her tears Rachel frowned at her. "But why? Why would he do that to me? My own father."

Ada shook her head. "I don't know, honey. I don't know."

Ada knew that Rachel had had no part in Gerald's trickery, but she also knew that by first telling the truth about Rachel's scheming to take Steve away from Alice, he had made his eventual lie seem plausible. And how to explain that to the judge?

Ada felt sorry for Rachel. The man she had idolized had turned out to be such a disappointment to her. God knows Ada had warned Rachel over and over that her father was not some white knight but an immature, selfish man who hadn't been able to face up to the responsibilities of a wife and baby and so had run out on them. In effect, he was doing the same today.

"What am I going to do?" Rachel wailed.

Sam stepped in. "You'll have to take the stand," he said, "and try to counteract his testimony." He shook his head, in confusion. "What I don't understand is what he said to you on the phone—that he'd come and testify for you. And then this."

Rachel wiped her eyes with the back of her hand. "I don't understand any of it. Not any of it at all."

"Rachel," Ada said, "come on in the ladies' room with me. Fix your makeup."

"Yes," Sam said, "that's a good idea."

When they came back out it was almost time to go back to the courtroom, but Rachel did look more composed, and she had put on fresh lipstick. "Look, Rachel," Sam said, "try to forget about your father and what he's saying. The judge is the one who's going to make the ruling. He's the one who's going to decide who's lying and who's telling the truth. If you jump up and start screaming again, he may think you're doing that because you know your father is telling the truth and you can't stand listening to it."

Rachel stared at Sam in shocked disbelief. "Sam, he's not telling the truth."

Sam rolled his eyes heavenward. "I didn't say he was. I'm just trying to explain to you how it could look to the judge. This isn't the first time I've been in a courtroom, Rachel. I know the tactics some people resort to. And the judge has had even more exposure to it than I have. Okay?"

"All right," she said, calming down.

Her mother squeezed her hand. "Sam's right, honey. You do what he says."

"All right," Rachel said again.

Once inside the courtroom, Ada left Sam and Rachel to return to where she'd been sitting. She gave Rachel's hand a final squeeze. "Take it easy, honey."

Rachel nodded. "Yeah, Mom. Okay."

Ada watched as the other spectators returned to their seats. As sorry as she felt for Rachel, she felt just as sorry for Alice and her family. As much as Ada longed for Rachel to find happiness and peace of mind, she had never wanted her to find it at Alice's expense, and she didn't want that now.

The court session reconvened, Gerald Davis returned to the witness stand, and John resumed his questioning.

"I want to get back to an earlier question, Mr. Davis," he began. "You stated that when Rachel tired of the agreement regulating Steven Frame's visits to their son, she prevented him from seeing the boy by avoiding all contact with him—refusing to return his phone calls, et cetera."

"Yes," Gerald said, "that's right."

"And by this tactic she hoped to meet with Steve herself."

"That's right."

John frowned at him. "How? How did she hope to achieve that meeting by using such a tactic?"

Gerald gave John an impatient look. "I've already told you. Steve was angry that she was avoiding him, and she knew it. I knew it myself. I took some of his phone calls. She told me if he got angry enough, and then she called him and suggested they get together and talk about Jamie, he'd do it. And he did. He did exactly that."

Rachel spun around to Sam, but before she could say anything he whispered, "Keep your voice down."

She nodded and did so. "He's telling it backwards again. It was his idea that I not talk to Steve. He was the one who said if Steve got angry enough he'd agree to meet with me." She rubbed a hand across her face. "Oh, why is he doing this to me?"

Sam squeezed her hand. "Take it easy, Rachel. You'll get your turn up there."

John had been checking his notes again. Now he said, "All right, Mr. Davis. Now we come to the night of the phone call. Will you tell us about that in your own words, please?"

Gerald looked puzzled. "Which phone call are you talking about? Rachel's call to Steve or my call to the hospital?"

"I'm sorry," John said, making a note on his pad. "We'll talk about both of them. In the order they happened."

"Okay," Gerald said. "The first one was Rachel's call to Steve—to say she wanted to meet with him to talk about his seeing Jamie, and why didn't she come to his office around five o'clock or so that evening. He said okay."

"All right," John said. "And then?"

"Then I called the hospital and spoke to one of the nurses on the station where Alice worked. I said I was calling for Alice's husband, Steve Frame, and that he wanted her to come pick him up at his office when she went off duty. The nurse said she would give Alice the message, and that was that."

Again John checked his notes. "And the purpose of that phone call, that message?"

For the first time since taking the stand Gerald looked at Steve, but Steve was self-consciously looking through a folder of notes in front of him on the plaintiff's table. Gerald turned back to John and answered the question. "Rachel was going to try to get Steve to see her alone. We figured that would be easy, since he wouldn't want anybody to know he was with her. Then she was going to try to fix it so that when Alice got there, she and Steve would be talking about something personal—to give Alice the impression that Steve still cared for Rachel."

At the defense table Rachel muttered, "He did still care for me. And he still does."

"Keep it down, Rachel," Sam warned in a whisper.

From her seat in the spectators' section, Mary Matthews turned to her husband. "If Steve didn't still care for Rachel, Jim, why did he agree to meet with her alone? Why didn't he insist on somebody else being there, to prevent what happened from happening?"

"Darling," he said, his voice as low as hers had been, "he was in his office when she called. He probably had his mind on half a dozen other things, and it simply didn't occur to him."

Mary, who had been unable to forgive Steve for what she regarded as his second transgression against Alice, made a face and said, "You always stand up for him, no matter what."

"Mr. Davis," John said, continuing his questioning after stepping to the plaintiff's table for a sip of water, "when you stated that Rachel was going to try to get Steve to see her alone, you used the word 'we.' 'We figured that would be easy,' you said. May I ask who you mean by 'we'?"

Gerald looked at John as if he were dense. "Rachel and me," he said. "Who else?"

"You and Rachel plotted this out together?"

"That's right."

John frowned at him. "Why? I mean, what was your interest in all of this, in seeing Steve's marriage to Alice broken up?"

Gerald shrugged and shifted in his chair on the witness stand. "I didn't have any interest in it. But Rachel was set on it, and she kept pestering me to do something about it for her. So I finally did."

Rachel pounded the defense table with her fist, then buried her face in her hands. "That's not so," she said in a fierce whisper. "That's not how it happened at all. Oh, what did I ever do to deserve this from him?"

Sam touched her shoulder. "Ssh, Rachel. Hold tight. It'll be our turn soon."

Checking his notes again, John said, "Just one or two more questions, Mr. Davis. Did Alice go to pick Steve up at his office?"

Sam stood up. "Objection. The witness has no firsthand knowledge of that."

"I'll withdraw the question," John said before the judge could rule. "Let me ask you this, Mr. Davis. Do you know whether or not the plot you and Rachel put together had the desired effect of breaking up the marriage of Alice and Steven Frame?"

Gerald shrugged again. "I know Alice left Steve that same night. And she didn't come back."

John nodded and turned to the judge, saying, "I have no further questions of this witness." He left his place before the witness stand and sat down at the plaintiff's table beside Steve, who flashed him a grateful look before returning to his folder of notes.

The judge turned to Sam, and Sam got up, picking up the pad he'd been making notes on. With a final warning glance at Rachel, who was stirring restlessly in her seat again, he walked to the witness stand. "Mr.

Davis," he said, "you stated earlier that your daughter, Rachel, came to the conclusion that her husband, Ted Clark, was a loser, and you agreed with her."

"That's right."

"Wasn't it in fact the other way around? You reached the conclusion that Ted Clark was a loser and then set about persuading Rachel he was?"

Gerald shook his head. "No. That's not how I remember it. It was the way I said it was. It came from her. I mean, what difference would it make to me if he was a loser or not?"

"Considering he was managing a restaurant you had invested money in, I'd think it would make a lot of difference to you."

He shook his head again. "Not with me there to keep an eye on how he managed it."

Sam wanted to impress the judge with the conflicting statements, so he walked back to the defense table as if to get another note, gave the restlessly stirring Rachel another warning glance, then returned to the witness stand. Checking his notes, he continued, "Later on in Mr. Randolph's examination, in reference to the time when Rachel prevented Steve from seeing Jamie, you stated that it was Rachel's idea to avoid talking to Steve on the phone—in the hope he would get angry enough that he would agree to meet with her."

Gerald nodded. "That's right. It was."

"Was it?" Sam countered, frowning. "Was it not in fact your own idea? Wasn't it you who told Rachel that if Steve got angry enough he would agree to meet with her?"

Gerald ran a finger around the inside of his shirt collar, as if it were too tight. "I hardly knew Steve Frame," he answered. "I hardly know him now. How would I know what would make him do something or not do it? No. You've got it backwards. It was Rachel's idea. All I did was go along with it, that's all."

Hearing some small sound behind him, Sam turned to look at Rachel. She seemed more and more agitated, so he walked back to the defense table and poured himself a glass of water. After taking a sip, he said to her, "Sit tight now. No outbursts, please," then returned to the witness stand.

"Mr. Davis," he said, resuming his cross-examination, "you have stated here—and I'll remind you that you're under oath, and that perjury is a criminal offense—you have sworn that Rachel plotted with you in making the phone call to the hospital to leave the message for Alice. In fact, she knew nothing about that phone call until many months later, when you told her what you had done. Isn't that true?"

Rachel's father shook his head. "No, that's not true. She was in on it with me from the start."

Sam frowned. "I'll remind you once again you're under oath—and that the penalty for perjury is imprisonment."

Gerald gave Sam a malicious look, and when he spoke it was in a tone of voice to match. "I don't need your reminder, and if I'd known then I was going to end up in this courtroom having to testify about it, I never would have let her talk me into doing it."

"That's a lie!" Rachel shouted. She jumped to her feet. And looked straight at her father, who still wouldn't look at her. "I never did any such thing! You're lying!" Unable to get any response from her father, not even a look in her direction, Rachel turned to the judge. "He's lying, I tell you! My father is lying!"

There was a commotion in the courtroom as

everybody started talking about Rachel's outbursts. Mary Matthews turned to her husband, Jim. "Rachel can't bear to listen to the truth."

"Hush, darling," Jim said. "Keep your voice down or the judge will order the courtroom cleared."

But the hubbub continued.

Ada had nobody to comment to. She listened to what was being said around her, and though she knew Gerald was lying, few others seemed to feel that way. She shook her head in sadness, almost in despair.

When the hubbub didn't die down on its own, the judge rapped on his bench. "Order. Order. This court will come to order."

Sam was already at Rachel's side trying to calm her down, but she had burst into tears again, and she shook him off time and again.

Sam looked at the judge in mute appeal, and the judge nodded. "All right," he said. "We'll take another fifteen-minute recess."

The bailiff said, "All rise," and as they did the judge got up and left the courtroom.

The moment he was out of the room Rachel darted to the witness stand, which her father was getting ready to leave. "How could you?" she shouted at him. "How could you lie like that?"

He looked at her with no expression on his face. "I'm not lying."

She waved a fist at him. "You are! You know you are!"

He shook his head. "Rachel, you wouldn't know the truth if it came along and bit you. You've been telling lies all your life, so who are you to say I'm lying?"

Few of the spectators had left the courtroom. Most of those who had risen sat back down and listened to this confrontation between Rachel and her father.

"How could you do this to me?" she was saying. "How could you?" For a moment she simply stood there, trembling all over; then, as if a thought had just now struck her, she turned to look at Steve, still sitting with John at the plaintiff's table, then spun back to her father. "Steve paid you to lie for him, didn't he?"

There was an absolute stillness in the courtroom.

"No," Gerald said.

Rachel stared at him. "It has to be that. There isn't any other answer. He paid you."

Her father spread his hands. "If you want to believe that, go ahead and believe it."

Tears ran down her face. "My own father," she said in a disbelieving voice. "My own flesh and blood. A man I've loved all my life. Never mind that you walked out on Mom and me before I was even old enough to know you. Never mind you didn't ever bother to get in touch with either of us. I loved you in spite of that. In spite of everything. I dreamed about you, and I looked for you. I did everything I could to find you, and I found you. And I went on loving you, even when you treated me like dirt."

The stillness in the courtroom was absolute, all eyes and ears on Rachel and her father.

"Yes," she said. "Like dirt. But I still went on loving you. And then you came to Bay City to live, and I thought things were finally going to work out for you and me. We were running that restaurant together, and we became closer than we ever had before, and you acted like you loved me. I really thought you did. And now this." She waved a hand to encompass the courtroom. "Now you sit here in this room, and you tell lies about me, and for what? Because you like Steve Frame? Because you think he's such a great man, after the way he treated you? You'd wipe your feet on him if you could. But if he offers you some money—to see your lying, cheating soul—why you don't mind doing *that*."

By now Rachel's voice had become quite shrill. "Mind doing it? You'll be *happy* to do it. And what does it matter that you'll destroy your own daughter in the process? Oh, I never want to see you again in my life. Never!"

Sobbing, she turned and ran out of the courtroom. And what had been a stillness became an elongated sigh as the spectators turned to one another, aghast at what they had just witnessed.

Chapter Six
For Jamie's Sake

As Ada left the courtroom to go after Rachel, Sam hurried up the aisle with the same object in mind. Meanwhile, Gerald Davis stepped over to the plaintiff's table, where John and Steve sat. "Do you need anything more out of me?" he asked.

John shook his head. "I don't think so." He held a hand up. "But there's always the possibility of a redirect. If you want to wait in an anteroom outside the courtroom—"

"I know where it is," Gerald said. "I was waiting there before."

Making his way to it, he walked past Rachel and Ada and Sam. He gave no indication that he saw them there, and they stood silent, watching him until he disappeared.

Ada put an arm around Rachel. "Try and put it all behind you, honey." She shook her head. "I don't know what else you can do."

"Well, I do," Sam said. "She can say he was lying." He turned to Rachel. "Do you want me to ask the judge to extend the recess another ten or fifteen minutes?"

The confrontation with her father had drained Rachel of all emotion. "No," she said in a listless tone of voice.

He frowned. "Are you sure? Unless we get lucky, and the judge orders a continuation, you're going to have to take the stand sometime this afternoon."

She nodded. "I know that."

His frown deepened. "Will you be all right?"

She shrugged. "Yes, I'm all right." Her voice was still listless, her manner withdrawn, her body limp. She looked up at Sam. "It's all over, Sam, isn't it?"

"No," he said, though he believed it was. But they still had to try. "Rachel," he said beseechingly, "you've got to pull yourself together. Put some more makeup on. Get some color back in your face. Straighten your shoulders. Hold your head up. You can't win something if you come across looking and sounding like you've already lost."

Ada joined the plea. Squeezing Rachel to her, she said, "Honey, Sam's right."

"All right," Rachel said. "Just give me a few minutes by myself."

She headed once more for the ladies' room. Sam and Ada watched her go; they looked at each other with not much hope in their faces, then turned and made their way back into the courtroom.

A few minutes before the recess was due to end, Rachel joined Sam at the defense table. She had put on fresh makeup, and she looked considerably better, but she still seemed down. He gave her hand an encouraging squeeze and hoped she would bounce back before she had to testify.

When the court reconvened Sam told the judge he

had no further questions for Gerald Davis. John then called to the stand the nurse who had taken Gerald's phone call, merely to confirm the fact. Sam had no questions to ask her, so John next called Alice to the stand.

Alice looked almost as pale as Rachel had after her confrontation with her father. She had been almost as badly shaken by it as Rachel herself.

John smiled at her. "I have only a few questions," he said.

She glanced at Steven. He smiled at her—it was their first eye contact of the afternoon, each of them bending over backward not to seem aware of the other's presence—but she did not smile back, just settled into the witness chair more comfortably.

Checking his notes, John said, "You've heard the nurse's testimony about the phone call."

"Yes."

"Do you recall getting the message that was in that phone call?"

She nodded. "Yes. The message was that Steven had called—or, rather, somebody had called *for* him, asking me to meet him at his office when I went off duty."

"And did you do that?"

"Yes."

"Will you tell us in your own words what happened?"

"Yes. When I got to his office, somebody who was just leaving said Steve had gone out for a while, so I sat down to wait. Then I heard sounds from his apartment overhead, and I went up there, thinking that was where he must be."

She was silent for a moment, and when she spoke again there was sadness in her voice. "He was there with Rachel. I stood listening to them—they didn't know I was there—and I heard Rachel say she was with Steven the day I lost—"

Alice broke off, then swallowed and began again. "I had been pregnant and miscarried. I heard Rachel say she was with my husband when that happened. I also heard" —she swallowed again— "I also heard some other things I misinterpreted, things that led me to believe Rachel and Steven were . . . were having a continuous relationship. And so I didn't stay to hear any more. It was too painful. I . . . I left."

"Left the apartment?"

"The apartment, the building, Bay City, my husband. I left them all. That same night."

"Your marriage was over?"

Alice swallowed dryly. "Yes. My marriage was over."

"Because of what you had overheard? Because of what it led you to believe?"

"Yes. That's right."

John nodded, and said to the judge, "I have no further questions of this witness."

The judge turned to Sam. Sam shook his head. As the judge dismissed Alice, John said, "I have no further witnesses."

It was now Sam's turn to present his case. Rachel was his only witness, and he called her to the stand. He took plenty of time asking her the routine opening questions, hoping that she would become relaxed and comfortable and ready for the tough questions ahead of them.

The tough questions began with her marriage to Ted Clark. "Was the marriage a happy one?" he asked.

She lifted her chin. "Yes," she answered in a firm, clear voice. "It was. Ted and I were very happy. We were so happy he even wanted to adopt Jamie. So we could be a real family."

"And how did you feel about his adopting Jamie?"

"I was all for it," she said in that same clear voice—and a number of spectators exchanged glances. "I thought it was a good idea. After all, at that time Jamie thought Ted *was* his father. Why not make it for real?"

There were more glances and a few whispers exchanged in the spectators' section, and at the plaintiff's table Steve said in a low voice to John, "Now the lies begin. Ted adopting Jamie was the last thing in the world she wanted. She is really something, Rachel is."

"Did the adoption go through?" Sam was asking.

Rachel shook her head. "No, it didn't. My husband—my present husband, Steven Frame—he's Jamie's real father—he objected to Jamie being adopted by somebody else. My husband—my present husband—had always been very close to our son. Very close to him and very proud of him."

Talking about Jamie and Steve had brought some of Rachel's animation back to her voice, and she sat up straighter in the witness chair. Sam began to feel more hopeful. "And what was your own position regarding the adoption?"

"Well," Rachel said, "naturally I wanted what was best for Jamie. I mean, all the rest of us who were involved were grown-up people who could look out for ourselves, but I felt Jamie needed protection, and so when Jamie's father—my present husband—objected so strongly, I felt I had to go along with him."

After the last recess Pat Randolph had moved from her mother's side to sit with Alice. She turned to her now and muttered, "If Rachel says 'my present husband' one more time I may scream."

Alice nodded and murmured back to her, "Let's hope this afternoon will be her last opportunity to call him that."

Sam checked his notes, then said, "Now Rachel, what happened to turn your happy marriage to Ted Clark into a not-so-happy one?"

She sighed. "When Ted went to prison for—well, for stealing some drugs—my father came to Bay City to help me run the Hearthside Inn. He began running Ted down to me then, and after Ted got out of prison and they were both there at the restaurant together, he started doing it even more. Until he finally got me to agree with him."

Sam checked his notes again. "Your father testified earlier this afternoon that your dissatisfaction with Ted Clark began with you."

She nodded. "I know that's what he said. But it isn't true. I was perfectly satisfied with Ted until my father started in on him."

"Then it's not true that you had designs on Steven Frame? That you wanted his marriage to Alice Matthews Frame broken up?"

"No, it's not true at all," she said vigorously. "I didn't have any designs on him."

Sam pressed on. "And the charge that you used your son to try to see Steve? To be alone with him?"

Rachel shook her head. "That's not true either. I mean, yes, I did see Steve from time to time about Jamie. I had to see him about Jamie. There were things we had to discuss about him, the way all parents do about their children. But that's all there was to it."

"You weren't trying to insinuate yourself into his good graces?" Rachel gave him such an uncomprehending look that Sam rephrased the question. "You weren't trying to make time with him for yourself?"

"Oh," she said. "No."

Sam walked to the defense table and poured himself a glass of water, swallowed some of it, and returned to the witness stand. "When your marriage to Ted Clark began to turn sour, at that time did you develop an interest in Steve Frame?"

She shook her head again. "No. I didn't become interested in Steve Frame, or have anything to do with him other than talk to him about Jamie, until after Alice—until after his wife had left him and he knew she wasn't coming back."

"Then you had nothing to do with the breakup of his marriage to Alice Matthews Frame?"

"No. Nothing."

"You didn't scheme to find ways to be with him?"

"No."

"You didn't plot with your father to have his wife find the two of you alone together in the hope it would break up his marriage to her?"

Again Rachel shook her head. "No. I knew nothing about that phone call he made—nothing. Not until he told me about it himself months and months later. If I'd known about it at the time I wouldn't have let him make the phone call, and that's what I told him when he finally did tell me what he'd done. I said it was a dumb thing to do."

"Rachel, your father said you did know he was making the call. He swore under oath you did."

Rachel's eyes didn't waver from Sam's face. "He was lying."

"Why?" Sam asked her. "Why did he lie?"

"Objection," John said, standing up.

Sam held up a hand. "All right. I'll rephrase the

question. Rachel, why do you think your father was lying?"

Rachel gave Sam a look of defeat. "I don't know. I just don't know. Maybe—" She broke off and looked over at Steve, who was watching her intently. If she had intended accusing him of paying her father to lie for him, she changed her mind. Turning back to Sam, she said again, "I don't know."

Sam turned to the judge. "I have no further questions of this witness."

Sam sat back down at the defense table, and John approached the stand to begin his cross-examination. It was much like Sam's examination had been. Rachel denied conspiring with her father to break up Steve's marriage to Alice, but she also denied—and with just as much intensity—that she had schemed in any way to break the marriage up. Yet the majority of the spectators in the courtroom had heard Rachel say—and more than once—that Steve belonged to her, not Alice; that she intended taking him away from her.

Once again she may have intended to accuse Steve of paying her father to lie for him, but if so, she changed her mind, merely repeating that she didn't know why her father had lied.

When it came time for the judge's ruling, he ruled in favor of Steve. Rachel and Steve were to be divorced.

Disappointed—bitterly so—Rachel left the court-room. Once outside it, she said to her mother what she hadn't had the nerve to say inside. Turning to Ada in the corridor, she said, "Steve paid him to do it. I know he did."

Ada shook her head. "Honey," she said, "you don't know anything of the kind. You can believe it. I could even believe it myself. But you don't know it for a fact."

Rachel tossed her head. "My father would do anything for money. Or almost anything. He certainly wouldn't hesitate to do what he did to me if Steve paid him enough." She sighed. "Oh, Mom, if only I'd listened to you all those years ago. If only I hadn't gone chasing after my father," she said, rather dismayed.

Ada was shocked to hear Rachel say that. Rachel was not one to admit to making a mistake. Ada said nothing about it, though. All she said was, "It's too late for that now, Rachel. Way too late."

"I know it is," Rachel agreed. "It's too late for anything." She looked up as the members of the Matthews family came out of the courtroom, Steve and Alice in the middle of the group. She watched them pass by and walk on out of the courthouse. "I suppose he'll marry Alice again now."

Her mother frowned at her. "Honey, that's what this was all about."

"Yeah," Rachel said, looking at the door through which the victorious family had passed, "Well, it's not going to be as easy as they think."

Ada stared at her in horror. "Rachel, you just admitted you wish you had listened to what I said about your father all those years ago. Listen now to what I say about Steve Frame. Forget him. Put him out of your mind. It's over."

Rachel shook her head. "No, it's not over, Mom. Not by a long shot."

A few days after Steve's divorce was granted, the judge summoned Steve and Rachel to the courthouse, asking for Jamie to be there as well. He took Jamie alone with him into his chambers.

Jamie, now seven years old, had witnessed more than his father kissing Alice at Lenore's house. He had seen the tension between his parents before Steve moved out of the house, had overheard them quarreling. In particular he had heard his mother tell Ada that she was not going to let Steve run out on her the way Ada had let Gerald run out on them. Let Steve say he didn't care about her anymore. She was going to fight to keep him, for Jamie's sake. All that she was doing, she was doing for his sake.

That was the burden Jamie brought with him into the judge's chambers the day custody was to be decided. Or, as the judge put it to Jamie as they sat together in his office, "We have to decide now what happens to you, Jamie."

Jamie shrugged his thin shoulders and said, "I don't care what happens to me."

The judge spoke as gently as he could. "You mustn't say that, Jamie. The rest of us care what happens to you. We care very much."

Jamie looked at him. "My father doesn't care."

Disturbed at that remark, the judge frowned. "What makes you think that?"

The little boy shrugged again. "He left me, didn't he?"

The judge held out his arms to Jamie. "Come here, son." He put his arm around the boy and pulled him closer. "Your father didn't leave you, Jamie. He and your mother decided they didn't want to live together any longer, and—"

"No," Jamie said, interrupting him. "My mother didn't decide that. My mother loves my father. She didn't want him to leave. She said so. I heard her say it."

"Well," the judge said, "your father decided he didn't

want to stay married to your mother, and when somebody makes a decision like that, then one of the two people—usually the father—moves out of the house the family has been living in and goes to live by himself somewhere. And that's what your father did."

Jamie looked at the judge's shirt cuffs sticking out from under his robe. "And it's all my fault, isn't it?"

"No, Jamie, no. It doesn't have anything to do with you," the judge reassured the young boy.

"But my mother said—I heard her say it—she said she didn't want my father to leave, and it was all because of me."

The judge shook his head. "Jamie, your parents both love you. Each of them wants you to live with them. It's because your father no longer wanted to live with your *mother* that he divorced her."

Jamie stood silently digesting that. Finally he said, "You mean it's all his fault?"

The judge put a finger under Jamie's chin to make the boy look at him. Gently he said, "Why don't we say it's nobody's fault?"

Again Jamie turned silent. Finally he nodded and said, "All right," but he didn't say it with any conviction.

Once again the judge put his finger under Jamie's chin. "Now I want you to tell me how you feel about your parents. How do you feel about your mother?"

"I love her."

"And how do you feel about your father?"

Jamie stared at the shirt cuffs again. "I don't know."

"Do you love him?"

Jamie resembled his mother more than he did his father, and he had adopted one of her habits—sticking his chin up in a gesture of defiance. He stuck it up now and said, "He doesn't love me."

The judge frowned. "But I just told you a minute ago he does. He's told me so himself."

Jamie shook his head. "That's what he says, but I don't believe him, because if he loved me he wouldn't have left."

And try as the judge might, he couldn't budge Jamie from that position. Asking his clerk to take Jamie out to his grandmother, the judge had Steve and Rachel brought in, each accompanied by counsel. Sam had warned Rachel not to erupt into any emotional outbursts or she might lose custody of Jamie. She sat quietly, and when the judge awarded custody to her she only nodded.

The judge turned to Steve. "Jamie doesn't understand why his parents have divorced. First he thought it was his fault. Now he thinks it's yours. I tried to explain things to him, to make him understand it's nobody fault—"

At that Rachel began stirring, but Sam put a warning hand on her arm.

"—but he's too young to understand this situation."

"I realize that," Steve said.

The judge settled back in his chair, a disturbed look on his face. "What I can't talk him out of, Mr. Frame, is his feeling that you don't love him." He put up a hand to prevent Steve from interrupting. "Now, I understand that it's irrational, but his feeling—and it's a typical one for a child in this situation—is that if you loved him you wouldn't have left him." He put his hand up again. "I'm telling you this so you'll understand what you have to deal with, because I want you to have visitation rights, but I can't force Jamie to see you."

Steve frowned. "What does that mean?"

The judge shrugged. "It means what I said. Most children are distressed when the family breaks up. I don't want this child's distress exacerbated by forcing him to spend time with you if he doesn't want to do it of his own volition."

"I'm sure that, left alone, I can convince him that I love him," Steve said.

"That may be," the judge agreed.

"What I'm not so sure of," Steve went on to say, "is that his mother won't work to turn him more against me than he already is." His jaw was clenched.

The judge swiveled his chair around to Rachel. "Have you given your former husband reason to feel this way?"

Her chin went up. "No, I have not."

John stood up. "Your Honor, if you'll recall the divorce hearing, testimony was given about the time Rachel kept Steve from seeing Jamie altogether for an extended period of time, even though she had signed an agreement spelling out his visitation rights."

Rachel glared at John, then quickly cleared her face as the judge turned to her again. "I'm making it a position of this court that you must not influence your son against his father. I will add that if word comes to me of such influence I will call all parties to the dispute to these chambers and reconsider the custody agreement. Is that understood?"

Rachel was flushed. She nodded, and said, "Yes."

The judge dismissed them, and they filed out of his chambers. Steve went to the anteroom where Jamie waited with Ada. He put a hand on Jamie's arm, but Jamie twisted away from him, crying out, "Don't touch me! Don't touch me!"

"Son," Steve said, trying to appeal to him.

"No," Jamie said, shaking his head. He clung to his grandmother, who looked as distressed as Steve. "Where's my mother?"

Rachel entered the anteroom. "I'm right here, darling." She took Jamie's hand in hers. "Come along now. We're going home." She flashed a look of triumph at Steve.

"Don't forget what the judge told you," he said.

Rachel turned to her mother. "Mom, take Jamie outside for a minute and wait for me there. I'll be right out, Jamie."

"Okay," he said, and went out with Ada.

Rachel turned back to Steve, a set look on her still-flushed face. "I won't forget what the judge told me. But you see to it that *you* don't do something to make us all have to come back here."

Steve frowned in puzzlement. "I don't know what you're talking about."

She folded her arms across her chest. "Don't try to pay somebody off, Steve, to get Jamie away from me."

"Are you crazy? Why would I do something like that?"

"You paid my father off, didn't you, to testify against me at the hearing?"

"Don't be ridiculous."

Rachel had been holding herself in check since before the custody hearing in the judge's chambers. Now she lashed out. "You're lying the same as he did. You think you can buy your way out of anything, but you'll find out." She turned to a corner of the room where the two lawyers had been talking together. "Sam, what did you tell me lying on the stand is?"

He looked at John and looked away again. "Perjury."

"And what did you say John would have to do if he

knew my father was guilty of that?"

Sam glanced at John. "I said he would be bound to inform the court."

John frowned first at Sam and then at Rachel. "Are you accusing your father, Rachel, of committing perjury?"

"That's right. I am. And I'm doing more than that. I'm accusing Steve of paying my father to do it."

"That's a serious charge, Rachel."

She didn't take her eyes from his face. "What other reason would my father have to come all the way from San Francisco and say what he said?"

Steve answered her. "He came to right a wrong, Rachel."

She made a mocking face. "Oh, sure. Well, call it whatever you want to call it, but I didn't have any part in what my father did, and anyone who says I did is lying." She turned to John. "Why don't you find out whether I'm telling the truth or not? Unless you're in on it too?" Before he could answer her she turned to Sam. "Come on, Sam. Leave them to talk in private." And she pulled Sam out of the anteroom.

John didn't want to believe Rachel was telling the truth. For one thing, she was a notorious liar. For another, Steve was not only a client, he was a friend, and both Steve and Alice had been hurt by Rachel, with or without her father's help. Still, it had been troubling him that after the divorce hearing, Gerald Davis had not come to his office to pick up his expense money, and he mentioned that now to Steve.

Steve shrugged. "He probably forgot it."

John shook his head. "The last thing Gerald Davis would ever forget is money."

"Yes," Steve agreed. "Under ordinary circumstances.

But after that run-in with Rachel? That must have blown his mind."

"I suppose it could have," John said. "But Rachel isn't the only one to make these allegations, Steve. A lot of other people witnessed that scene between Rachel and her father. They think that for once Rachel was telling the truth."

"They can think what they like," Steve said with another shrug. "Now that I've gotten the divorce I could care less."

John stood there eyeing him. "Gotten it fair and square?"

Steve eyed him back. "Are you suggesting anything?"

"You gave me your word."

"Are you doubting it now?"

John stood silent for a moment, then he said, "I'll ask you straight out. Did you bribe Gerald Davis?"

Steve looked at John, flushed and angered. "Go to hell," he said, and turned and walked out of the room.

The next day John flew to San Francisco.

Chapter Seven
Father and Son

On the day Steve had his first afternoon with Jamie, Jamie had to be talked into going out with his father, a reluctance made plain by Jamie's attitude toward him.

It was a raw March day, with a biting wind. Father and son were both wearing faded jeans and thick wool red sweaters. As they walked along the shore of the bay in the public park at the south end of the city, Jamie kept his hands jammed in his pants pockets.

"Are you warm enough, son?" Steve asked as a fierce gust of wind swept in off the bay. "We can go inside somewhere if you're not."

"No," Jamie said. "I'm okay."

"Would you like something hot to drink? Cocoa, maybe? There's a stand along here somewhere that sells it."

"No."

For the next few minutes they trudged along the pathway in silence. Finally Steve said, "How's school?"

"Okay."

"You playing any Little League?"

"Yeah."

"Oh? What position?"

"Catcher."

"That's great, Jamie," Steve said with a smile. "Good catchers are hard to come by, you know."

"Yeah."

Steve tried another smile. "Is that all you can give me, son? Just one-word answers? We used to have some good conversations, you and I. Remember?"

"Yeah."

Steve looked down at his son. "That's all you have to say, Jamie? Yeah? It's hard to get a conversation going if all you're going to give me to work on is yeah or no or maybe."

Jamie wouldn't look at him. "Then let's don't talk at all."

Steve hunched his shoulders against the wind. "If that's the way you want it, son, then that's the way it'll be, I guess, but I'd hate to have this little time we get together be all silence."

Now Jamie looked at him—and almost immediately looked away. "If you hadn't left us we could be together all the time."

Steve hunched his shoulders again. The wind was getting colder. "I know," he said. "That was the hardest part of leaving—the fact that I had to leave you."

Again they trudged along in silence. Finally Jamie spoke up. "And what about Mom? Didn't you mind leaving her?"

"No," Steve said as gently as he could. "I wanted to leave your mother, Jamie."

"Why?"

"I shouldn't have married her in the first place."

Jamie frowned up at him. "But if you're my father,

and she's my mother, how could you not be married to her?" His eyes revealed his confusion.

"Jamie," Steve said with a sigh, "I know it's hard for you to understand, but someday, when you're older, maybe I can explain it to you so you will understand."

"Maybe," Jamie said without conviction.

"What does your mother say to you about it?"

"Nothing much." Now Jamie hunched his shoulders, too, maybe copying his father, maybe not. "But I hear her crying sometimes." He shook his head. "I don't like to hear her cry. Grown people shouldn't do that."

"I know, son. But they do sometimes." Steve was sorry he'd asked what Rachel had to say about all this, and he cast about for some way to change the subject.

Jamie looked up at him again. "She never cried till you left her."

"Maybe not." Another gust of wind swept in off the bay. Steve thought surely Jamie must be wanting something hot to drink now.

He was about to suggest it when Jamie said in a hopeful tone of voice, "If you came back I bet she'd stop." He became more positive, almost excited. "I bet she would. I'm sure of it. Why don't you come back and then we'll see?"

Steve couldn't let him go on. That would only get his hopes up higher—the farther to fall. "No, Jamie. I'm sorry, but that's not possible."

Jamie frowned at him. "Why isn't it?"

He tried again to explain. "Your mother and I— Jamie, we don't belong together. We never— Look, son, I know it's hard for you to understand, but—"

Jamie interrupted him. "You're going to marry the blond lady, aren't you?"

"Yes," Steve said. "I was married to her once before,

and I'm going to marry her again. Her name is Alice."

Jamie gave him a sullen look, reminding Steve of Rachel. "I know what her name is."

"You know more than her name, Jamie. You've met her several times. You like her."

Jamie shook his head. "No. Not anymore."

Steve frowned down at him. "Why not?"

"Because that's why my mother cries so much. Because you left her to marry Alice."

Steve hastened to correct him. "No, Jamie, that's not true. I would have left your mother whether I married Alice or not, so you mustn't blame Alice for my leaving your mother. Jamie, I want you to go back to liking Alice."

The little boy shook his head again. "No."

Another gust of wind swept in off the bay. The waters were choppier now and a deeper shade of gray. "After Alice and I are married," Steve said, "and we're back living in the house—"

Jamie interrupted him again. "You mean our house?"

Steve suppressed a sigh. "The house you and your mother and I lived in, yes. But Alice lived there first, Jamie. I built that house for her. So it's really her house."

"Oh."

"But," he hastened to add, "I'm sure Alice would want you to think of it as your house, and she'd want you to come there as often as you could—maybe even stay overnight sometimes."

"No," Jamie said. He stopped walking, and when Steve stopped too, he said, "Can you take me home now?"

"Are you cold?"

He shook his head. "No. I just want to go home."

"All right. Whatever you say. Let me see where we've

got to." He looked around, then pointed. "If we cut back this way, on the diagonal, it'll only be a short hike to the car."

"Okay," Jamie said.

They set off, heading directly into the wind now, both of them with their shoulders hunched. As they walked along Steve said, "Will you come see Alice and me after we're married?"

Jamie shook his head. "No. My mother wouldn't want me to."

"Has she said so?"

"No."

"Then what makes you think she wouldn't want you to?"

He shrugged. "I just know. And anyhow, I won't have time."

Steve wondered what Rachel had been saying to Jamie. He couldn't believe she hadn't said anything. "What do you mean, Jamie, you won't have time?"

Jamie was back to not looking at him, keeping his head down. "I have to stay home with my mom. She hasn't got anybody else now but me. And when I hear her crying in her room, if I go in, then she stops crying. So that's what I have to do."

Steve clenched his hands against the anger building up in him. If Rachel was crying it wasn't for love of him but for the effect it would have on Jamie—the effect it *was* having on him. He tried to sound calm. "Maybe you'll feel different in a while—about coming to see us, I mean."

"No," Jamie said, his head still down. "No, I won't."

"Jamie," Steve said. He put an arm around the boy's shoulders, but Jamie twisted away from him.

"I don't like you touching me," he said.

"Jamie . . ."

"No! Stay away. Stay away, I said." He started running, ran all the way back to the car.

Steve didn't try to stop him or keep up with him. He thought maybe the running would release Jamie's tension, and then they could get back together on their old terms. But he was wrong. When Steve got back to the car Jamie was sitting in the passenger seat up against the car door, as far away as he could get from the driver's seat. And he stayed that way all the way home.

Steve knew without asking that John had flown out to San Francisco. He didn't know what would happen once he got together with Gerald Davis, but he suspected the worst.

The evening of his unsuccessful outing with Jamie, Steve took Alice to dinner at one of his favorite French restaurants, down along the docks. After they finished eating they walked awhile along the piers. The area had at one time been allowed to deteriorate, but then a few years ago the city and private developers, Steve among them, had begun restoring the area, and now it was back to looking first-class.

The raw wind of that afternoon had died down, so the walk was a comfortable one.

"When is it the first day of spring?" Alice asked as they ambled along a pier used for flea markets.

Steve looked at her blankly for a moment, then shook his head. "Sorry, what was that you asked?"

Alice hesitated a few moments, then said gently, "Darling, you've been so quiet all evening."

He took her hand in his. "Have I?"

She smiled tenderly. "So much so, I wasn't sure you knew who you were with."

He put an arm around her and drew her close. "Not a chance of that."

She pulled away from him to look at him. "Then something's bothering you."

He nodded. "Many chances of that." He drew her close again, then released his hold on her. "We've got some rough times ahead, I'm afraid."

They had come to the end of the long pier, and they stood looking out across the bay, where the setting sun was turning water and sky glorious oranges, pinks, and purples. Alice turned from the sunset to look at Steve. "What's happening?"

"Nothing that I know of."

She frowned. "Then what do you mean about rough times? What were you referring to?"

"Oh . . . Jamie for one." He told her about their afternoon together—or not together.

Alice took his hands in hers. "Steven, he'll come around in time."

"I hope so."

"Darling, I'm sure of it. He's just so torn right now, and scared by his mother's crying. But Rachel will settle down in a bit, and then Jamie will too."

He nodded. "I guess you're right."

They turned and started back along the pier the way they had come. "What other rough times, Steven?" Alice asked.

"I don't know."

She turned to look at him, pulling him to a stop. "Don't know, or won't say?"

He gave her such a haunted look she almost cried out in pain. Then he stooped to pick up a flat stone and sailed it into the darkening waters. "What's that old saying? The one I never can remember, and never used to be able to understand until you explained it to me?"

She frowned again. "You mean 'Sufficient unto the day is the evil thereof'?"

"That's the one. Meaning, don't borrow more trouble than you've already got. Come on."

He took her hand and they continued their walk. It was beginning to get dark now.

"Alice," he said, stopping again, "do you want out?"

She stared at him, confused. "What do you mean?"

"What I said." He was looking at her intently, his dark, brooding eyes probing hers. "I don't know what's ahead for me—maybe bigger trouble than I've ever been in before. You don't have to be a part of it. I don't like asking you to be a part of it."

Her own gaze was steady, her blue eyes clear. "Do you want me out?"

"No," he answered. "But let's leave what I want aside for now. You're the one who stands to get hurt." He reached out to her and pulled her to him, holding her in a tight embrace. "Oh, God," he said over her shoulder, "I've hurt you so much already—you, the one person in this world I would least want to hurt."

She pulled back to look at him, to take his face in her hands. "Don't, Steven. Don't."

He kissed her—as fiercely and as passionately as he had ever kissed her. She responded with the same degree of passion. Abruptly he broke away from her, turned away from her. "I ask you if you want out," he said, his voice harsh, "and then I make it impossible for you to go. Or I try to, anyhow." He turned back to her. "Alice, go. Fast. Run away. Forget me. I'm not worth the heartbreak I bring you."

She stood absolutely still, looking at him, searching

his face. Then she held out her arms to him. "Steven. Darling."

He stood staring at her, then sighed and came back into her arms again. "Alice," he said hoarsely, "I love you with all my heart."

She nodded. "And I love you, Steven, with all of mine."

Once again they kissed, with as much passion as they had before, but this time when they broke apart, he grabbed her hand and said, "Come on. This is what the high school gym teacher advised for situations like this. Run."

Laughing, panting for breath, they ran back to the parking lot beside the restaurant, where he had left his Mercedes. There Alice said to him, "Look on the bright side."

"Okay," he agreed. "Point the way."

"I could still be living at home, and you'd have Mom to face when you brought me there."

He grinned. "By George, you're right."

Mary Matthews was so against the idea of Alice remarrying Steve that she had refused to take part in the champagne celebration when he won his divorce from Rachel. And any talk about Alice's upcoming wedding upset her.

"That's one thing you don't have to face," Alice said as she climbed into the car. "At least not now."

Climbing in on his side, Steve turned to her. "Maybe I won't have to face anything at all except a life of uninterrupted bliss."

Alice squeezed his hand. "There. You sound much better."

Starting the car, shifting into gear, and setting off for her apartment, he talked to her as if he didn't have a care in the world, but he wasn't fooling himself. And he doubted he was fooling Alice.

On his return to San Francisco Gerald Davis quit his job at the hamburger stand and, with the help of a local bank, parlayed his fifteen thousand dollars into the ownership of an established restaurant, living in an apartment above it. John found him there.

Gerald had hardly more than greeted John when he said, "You can tell Steve his story's safe with me."

"What story?" John said, frowning.

Gerald gave him a confused look. "Isn't that what Steve sent you out here to check up on? To make sure I was keeping my end of the bargain?"

John had been carrying his trench coat. Now he laid it over the back of a chair, but he remained standing. "Steve didn't send me out here," he said. "I came on my own. To see if he bribed you to testify to what you did. To what you and Rachel *supposedly* did together." On a nearby table lay publicity shots of the restaurant downstairs. Picking one up and looking at the red plush banquettes, the white lace curtains at the plate-glass windows, the white linen tablecloths on the tables, he shook his head. "I guess I could have saved myself the trip."

Gerald poured a drink and held it out to John, but John shook his head. After taking a swallow of it himself, he said, "I would have thought Steve would have leveled with you, you being his lawyer."

John shook his head again. "If Steve had leveled with me, you wouldn't have testified. I couldn't have allowed it."

Gerald took another swallow of his drink. "Well, then it's just as well you didn't know. Tell Steve I'm sorry I spilled the beans. It just never occurred to me you wouldn't be in on it." He nodded to the pictures on the table. "It's a nice place I got, don't you think?"

"Yes, it is," John agreed. "But I wouldn't count on keeping it if I were you."

Gerald gave him a belligerent look. "I'd like to know why not."

"You were warned at the hearing that perjury is a criminal offense."

Gerald relaxed. "Not if nobody finds out about it."

John shook his head again. "You don't seem to understand, Mr. Davis. I've found out about it. You've admitted it to me—almost without my asking."

"Well, to you, sure. But you're not going to say anything to anybody."

"What makes you think so?"

Gerald shrugged. "Common sense. You can't implicate me without implicating your own client—and your big buddy—Steve Frame. For all I know, it might even mean getting yourself in trouble."

"The only way I'll get in trouble is by sitting back and saying nothing, and I'm not going to let that happen."

Gerald gave him another belligerent look. "You mean you'd rat on Steve?"

John shrugged. "I'm going to ask Steve to go to the judge and tell him what he's done."

Gerald snorted. "Can you see a guy like Steve Frame doing that?"

"I don't know why not."

This time Gerald laughed aloud. "If you don't, then you know less than I'd give you credit for. If Steve went to the judge and told him what he did, do you think the judge would pat him on the head and congratulate him for being like little George Washington?"

"No."

"Isn't he more likely to send him to jail?"

"He could."

Gerald laughed again. "And you still think Steve is going to do what you ask?"

"If he doesn't," John replied, "then I have no choice but to do it myself."

"I don't know why you have to do anything at all."

"I wouldn't expect you to understand. But whether or not you and Steve care about the law, I do. I'm sworn to uphold it, not contravene it."

Gerald finished his drink. "Fancy legal talk," he said. "Tell Steve I'm doubly sorry now I spilled the beans."

At that point John picked up his trench coat and left, and caught the next flight back to Bay City. The next morning he went to see Steve in his office. Sitting in front of Steve's massive desk, he told him about his meeting with Gerald.

"All right," Steve admitted, getting up from his desk and starting to pace. "It was the only way I could get him to come here and testify for me."

"Tell lies for you, you mean."

Steve stopped pacing and turned to him. "I don't believe that."

"I have it on his word."

Steve frowned. "You take his word one time and don't take it another?"

John spread his hands. "Look, Steve. I've told you this before. A lot of the people who witnessed that scene in the courtroom between Rachel and her father think she was telling the truth. I think she was too. And why would Gerald Davis tell me he was lying on the stand if he wasn't, when he knows as well as you and I do the penalty for perjury?"

"I don't think Gerald Davis knows when he's lying and when he's not," Steve said with a shake of his head. "Rachel had to be in with him on that phone call. Why would Davis do something like that on his own?"

John stood up and turned to face Steve, leaning against the massive desk. "I don't know, and I didn't come here to speculate on that. I came here to tell you what you have to do."

Steve eyed John in speculation. "Yeah? What?"

"You have to go tell the judge what you've done."

Steve gave him a disbelieving look. "Fat chance."

John put his hands behind him to clench the edge of the desk, and said in his most persuasive tone of voice, "Steve, Gerald Davis isn't the only one who's committed a crime. You have too. Don't you see that? Now, if you go to the judge on your own, he may be lenient with you. He'll certainly be more lenient than he will if you're arrested and brought to him."

For a moment Steve stared at John. Buying time to think, he returned to his desk and sat down, and John went back to his seat. Steve shook his head again. "I don't intend to be arrested and brought to him."

A feeling of relief swept through John. "Then you'll go to him on your own?" But the feeling was short-lived.

"I haven't done anything to go to him about," Steve said.

"You bribed a man to commit perjury."

Steve faced John squarely. "I gave a man some money to open a new business. That same man also testified for me."

"Lied for you."

"Testified for me."

For a few moments John didn't answer. Then he got

up, and now he began pacing about Steve's office. "All right. You leave me no choice. If you won't go to the judge to tell him what you've done, then I have to go to him."

From his desk chair Steve gave John a beseeching look. "John, you don't *have* to do anything."

John shook his head. "Steve, you seem to think you're above the law—that the law only applies to other people, not to you. Well, so be it. But I happen to be one of those other people. If you won't go to the judge, I must."

Steve was beginning to get angry now. "If you do," he said, "then you can get yourself some other clients, because you won't be working for me any longer."

In any other situation John would have laughed. But Steve was a valued friend. He gave a resigned shake of his head and said, "I seem to be damned if I do and damned if I don't. Because if I don't go to the judge and this story comes out—as all stories do sooner or later— then I won't be able to work for you or anybody else. I'll be disbarred."

Steve left his desk and came over to where John stood. "Look," he said, sounding as reasonable as he could, "can't we work this thing out between us? Say Gerald Davis did lie, that Rachel had no part in that phone call he made to the hospital. Didn't she do everything else she could to try to break up my marriage to Alice?"

"Yes," John admitted, "she did."

"Then what's the difference?"

John shook his head again. "The difference is that the end doesn't justify the means. Steve, I'm sorry. We've been friends and business associates for a long time now. We've been through a lot together. But look at this thing from another point of view—from your *own* point of view."

"How do you think I've been looking at it?"

"That isn't what I mean. Say I did what you asked me. Say I kept quiet. Say we didn't even have to worry about Gerald Davis blackmailing us—which is something else I don't think has occurred to you."

"No," Steve admitted. "You're right. It hadn't."

"Don't think it hasn't occurred to *him*."

"Yeah, well . . ."

John nodded. "All right. Say—for whatever reason—we didn't have to worry about that. Now you think the whole business is behind you, right?"

Steve looked perplexed. "But it would be, John."

John shook his head again. "I haven't finished. Say something else comes up, something that has no bearing on this case whatever. Say somebody is injured on one of your construction sites and sues you for damages. I represent you. You lose the case."

Steve waited for John to continue. When he didn't, Steve said, "All right. So I lose the case. It won't be the first one I've lost."

"It will be the first one you've lost where you're not sure your own lawyer hasn't double-dealed behind your back."

Steve stared at John in open disbelief. "You?"

"Why not? If I kept quiet about you breaking the law, I could just as easily keep quiet about the facts in a case against you. Especially if your opponent made it worth my while."

Steve waved his arm in a gesture of dismissal. "That's ridiculous," he said.

"If the damages paid the injured party were enough—say, around a million—you might not brush it aside so easily, saying it's ridiculous. . . . Well?"

Again the gesture of dismissal as Steve walked back behind his desk. "You're talking about something that's not going to happen."

"That's right," John said, coming back to the chair he'd left. "And it's not going to happen because one of us—you or me—is going to tell the judge Gerald Davis was bribed to commit perjury."

The anger that had been rising and subsiding in Steve now exploded out of him as he slammed the desk with his hand. "You don't know that, damn it. It's his word against Rachel's."

John picked up his briefcase. "And his word against yours, Steve. If Gerald Davis wasn't lying on the stand, why did you have to pay him fifteen thousand dollars to say what he did?" The question rang true.

Steve had no answer for that. And it was clear John knew he had none. All he said was, "Oh, what's the use of arguing with you?"

"No use at all," John said, "because I've taken a stand, and I'm committed to it."

And with that, John strode out of Steve's office.

Even before John went to see the judge, his intention of doing so reverberated throughout Bay City, from one office to another, from one house and apartment to the next. Alice got angry with John because she was afraid that Steve's divorce from Rachel, about to become final, would instead be nullified.

Rachel had the same thought and got excited, but when she demanded that Sam go to the judge before John could, and turn both John and Steve in, and Sam refused, she then became angry at him. She accused him of wanting to see Alice and Steve married, and she said once again that she intended to keep that from happening and would do anything—anything at all—to see to it.

Pat Randolph got angry at both Steve and Alice for putting John between a rock and a hard place, and then she turned around and got angry at her own husband for allowing himself to be put there, irrational though that was. But then, Pat had two things to worry about—Alice and Steve's happiness, which she very much wanted, and John's livelihood, which she also very much wanted.

What none of them knew except John, was how ironic it all was. For when he met with the judge in his chambers, explaining that Gerald Davis had probably committed perjury, and that whether he had or not, Steve Frame had given him fifteen thousand dollars to testify for him, the judge said he probably would have granted Steve the divorce even without Gerald Davis's testimony.

After thanking John for coming to him, he instructed him to tell Steve not to leave Bay City.

Chapter Eight

Prisoner of Love

Steve was arrested and taken to the precinct house and booked like any ordinary criminal—fingerprinted, photographed, the works. He hadn't really believed John would go to the judge, so he was shocked as well as angry. He also got himself another lawyer.

The new man advised Steve to plead guilty with no defense, and that was what Steve did when he met with the judge in the judge's chambers. Then as soon as he was released on bail, he had all the documents regarding Steven Frame Enterprises removed from John's office.

Once that was done he went home to his penthouse apartment and waited there for Alice to join him when she got off from the hospital. It was a mild late-April day, but he was chilled to the bone, and he stayed that way even after Alice arrived.

Getting off the private elevator, she gave him an anxious look. "How did it go, darling?"

He took her coat and hung it up in the foyer closet. "I don't know. I thought I would, but I don't."

She frowned with concern. "You mean because you couldn't take it all in?"

"No." He led her to the chrome-and-black-leather sofa that so dominated his living room. "Sit down, Alice." He waved a hand to the bar. "Or maybe you'd like a drink."

"No, Steven. Not right now."

They sat down on the sofa together, she in her white nurse's uniform, he in a somber gray business suit—somber to match the look on his face, she thought. She squeezed his hand, alarmed to notice how cold it was. "Go on with what you were saying."

He shook his head. "Nothing has been decided, really. Except for one piece of good news. The divorce was made final."

Alice smiled and squeezed his hand again. "Oh, Steven. Oh, I'm glad for that."

"Yes," he said, "me too."

She gave him another anxious look. "And what about you?"

He shrugged. "What I told you before. I don't know. There'll be a hearing, but I don't know when. The judge didn't say, and my new attorney didn't ask." Steve shook his head again. "When John met with the judge to tell him what I'd done, he asked for leniency for me. I suppose now he wishes he hadn't." Steve had done more to John than dismiss him as his attorney. While Steve was in the precinct house being booked, John had gone there to see if he could be of help, and Steve had refused to see him or have anything to do with him.

"Oh, darling," Alice said now, "I don't think so. John isn't an avenging kind of person."

Steve sighed. "I wish I'd never gone to San Francisco

in the first place. He tried to talk me out of it. He said we could win the case without Gerald Davis, and I think now we could have. At least I wouldn't be in the fix I'm in."

Alice said the only thing she could say. "Darling, I'm sorry."

He hugged her to him. "Why should you be? None of this is your fault."

"Yes, it is. It's very much my fault. If I hadn't—"

He put a finger to her lips. "No, Alice, don't. What's done is done. It won't help either of us to try to remake the past. It can't be done."

Silence settled over them. At last she turned to him and said, "Will you make it up with John?"

He sighed again. "No. It's too late for that, too. First I wouldn't speak to him, and now he won't speak to me. And anyhow, it's all in the new lawyer's hands now." He looked at her with concern in his eyes. "What will that do to you and Pat?"

Alice shook her head. "I don't know. We'll have to work it out somehow." She smiled at him and squeezed his hand again. "But darling, don't you worry about that—with all the other things you have to think about."

Silence settled on them again, then he reached out to touch her hand. "Alice . . ."

She waited for him to go on. When he didn't, she prompted him. "Yes? What is it, Steven?"

He looked down at the hand he had touched. "Alice, you promised to marry me. I want to release you from that promise."

She searched his face. "Have you changed your mind about wanting to marry me?"

He looked away from her. "Would you believe me

if I said I have?"

"No." She reached out and touched his chin, turning his face so that he had to look at her. "No, Steven, I wouldn't believe you."

This time he searched her face, his dark, brooding eyes intent upon her. "All right. No, I haven't changed my mind, but I want you to change yours."

"Why, Steven, why?"

Sitting there in her white nurse's uniform, her face showing nothing but concern for him, she had never looked more vulnerable. He shook his head. "Alice," he said, pained for her, "I may have to go to prison. I probably will. There's a chance the judge will let me off with a fine, but I don't get that feeling." He shook his head again. "If I do go to prison, the record will always be there. The taint. You don't want to marry a convicted felon."

As he had put a finger to her lips before, she now put a finger to his. "Steven, stop talking that way. You are what you've always been to me. And what you'll go on being to me, whether you go to prison or not. And I not only still want to marry you, I want to marry you *now*."

He frowned at her. "Before the judge decides what he's going to do with me?"

"Yes. That's right. Now. Before the hearing."

His frown deepened. "But, Alice—what will people say?"

She shook her blond head. "I don't care what people say."

"But you have to care what *some* people say. Your mother, for instance. What about her?"

"I've already had it out with Mother."

Again he shook his head. "That must have been something."

Alice shrugged. "No, actually, it wasn't much of anything. Mom said she didn't think I ought to marry you, and I said I had no intention of changing my mind." Once again Alice reached out and took his hand in hers. "Steven," she said, her bright blue eyes intent upon him, "the happiest period of my life was when I was married to you before. I want that happiness back."

He pulled her to him again and held her close. "God knows I want to give it to you if I can."

She smiled at him. "You can. Now. Do you have a calendar?"

"I think so." He pulled away from her and reached into his pocket for his billfold. "There's one in here somewhere. Here." He took it out and handed it to her. "Why do you want a calendar?"

She grinned at him. "So we can pick a date for our wedding, silly. What else?"

He reached out to take the little plastic card from her. "Alice—"

She twisted away from him. "Steven, I mean it."

"What you mean is to be nice to me."

"No. I mean to make my life with you. Steven, these last few years have been agony for me. Do you want to prolong that?"

"No, of course I don't, but . . ."

"But what?"

He spread his hands in a gesture of futility. "I don't see how I can help prolonging it—whatever I do."

She touched his face. "Then trust me, darling, please."

At length he sighed. "All right."

"A fine thing," she said in mock disgust. "The bride was willing—nay, eager—but the groom had to be dragged, kicking and screaming, all the way to the church."

He smiled, trying to share her lightheartedness, but he still felt chilled inside.

While Alice and Steve bent over the little plastic calendar, trying to settle on a date for their wedding, Rachel was getting the news of Steve's guilty plea. She was sitting in her mother's kitchen, having a cup of afternoon coffee with her, when Sam came in, bringing with him the afternoon paper. He handed the paper to Rachel saying, "The story is there on the front page. Guilty as charged."

Rachel took the paper from him and eagerly scanned the story. "I was right," she chortled. "I knew I was." She turned to Ada. "Oh, Mom, isn't this the best news ever?"

Ada was at the stove, pouring Sam a cup of coffee. Now she handed it to him, and he sat down with the two of them. She turned to Rachel. "I don't know what you mean, best news ever." She looked at her young brother. "Unless you and Sam . . ."

Sam shook his dark head. "I don't know what she means either."

Rachel didn't hear either of them. She was now reading the story from beginning to end, and it was puzzling her. "I don't understand," she said, looking up with a frown. "What does this article mean, the divorce was granted? It's a mistake. It has to be. How could the judge grant the divorce when he has proof now my father was lying?"

Sam frowned back at her. "Rachel, the judge granted the divorce six weeks ago."

"Well, I know that. But it wasn't to be final until now.

And now that he knows the only way Steve was able to get it was by having my father lie for him, he should—" She appealed to Sam. "—whatever you call it."

"Revoke it."

"Yes. That's right."

"Well," Sam said, "should or shouldn't, he didn't."

Rachel glared at him. "What do you mean, he didn't? What did you say to him?"

"I didn't say anything to him, Rachel. The judge didn't consult me."

"Well, he should have."

Sam shook his head. "Tell that to him."

"All right. I will."

Rachel started to get up, but Sam pushed her back down. "Rachel, I was only joking. You're not going to tell the judge anything."

"I don't see why I can't."

"Because he'd throw you out of there. It's not any of your business."

She glared at him again. "If it's not my business, I'd like to know whose it is."

"It's his, Rachel. You had your say back in March at the hearing. After that it became the judge's business."

Rachel frowned at Sam in confusion. "But I just told you. The judge has proof now my father was lying."

Sam drank some of his coffee, already starting to cool. "Apparently that didn't make any difference. Apparently he felt Steve should have the divorce. Not apparently. Obviously. Or he wouldn't have let it go through."

Rachel threw down the paper. "It's not fair."

For the last few minutes Ada had been watching and listening, drinking her coffee, not saying anything. Now she turned to her ever-willful daughter. "Rachel, honey," she said in a placating tone of voice, "it is true, whether or not you're willing to admit it, that you did scheme to break up Steve and Alice's marriage."

Rachel now glared at her mother. "I did not."

Ada gave no ground. "The judge seems to think you did."

"Well, he's wrong."

Ada and Sam exchanged glances, and Sam tried to change the subject by talking about an upcoming case, but Rachel wasn't finished with what she had to say. She turned to Sam, cutting him off. "Steve will have to go to jail, won't he?"

"I don't know," Sam answered her. "That's something else the judge will have to decide."

"Well, I hope he does. And I hope he stays there awhile. A good long while."

Ada frowned at her. "Rachel, you've made such a production the last few months about wanting to stay married to Steve because of Jamie—and only because of Jamie. Why aren't you thinking about Jamie now?"

Rachel, never too quick to understand, frowned at her mother, once again confused. "What do you mean, why aren't I thinking about Jamie now? What does Jamie have to do with this?"

Ada shook her head in exasperation. "His father may be going to prison."

Rachel was still frowning at her mother. "Well? So?"

Ada sighed. "Don't you have the least concern how Jamie might feel about that? Of how he might be hurt by it?"

Rachel tossed her head. "Jamie doesn't care anything about his father anymore. He doesn't want to have anything to do with him."

Ada was more exasperated than ever. "That's what

Jamie *says*, Rachel. That has nothing to do with how he *feels*."

"He feels his father has abandoned him, which is exactly what his father has done."

Ada nodded. "Yes, and if Jamie really didn't care anything about his father—as you seem to think he doesn't—then Jamie could care less that his father abandoned him."

Rachel's answer to that was predictable. "Oh," she said, "you always take everybody's side but mine." She turned from her mother to Sam. "At least if Steve goes to jail he can't marry Alice."

"Why not?" Sam said.

"Well, for one thing, Alice wouldn't do it. And even if she would, how can you get married when you're in jail?"

"There's nothing to keep them from getting married now—before he has his hearing."

"Well," Rachel retorted, "they won't."

Rachel thought she'd had the last word, but she hadn't. A couple of weeks later, on a bright, warm day in early May, Steve and Alice were remarried where they had been married the first time—on the brick terrace of their big white house out in the country.

Rachel was livid when she heard the news. The morning of the wedding Ada tried to get Rachel to go out to lunch with her and then to a movie—to try to take her mind off what was happening—but Rachel wouldn't go. She stayed home alone, staring out one of the windows of her apartment, saying over and over how unfair it was.

Nor was she finished with Steve. He might think he was finished with her, but he'd find out one of these days how wrong he was, because she was going to take him away from Alice again.

She didn't know exactly how she was going to do it, but then, she hadn't known the first time exactly how she would do it either. She had simply hung in there, scheming and taking advantage where she could. And that was what she would do again. In spite of the fact that by marrying Alice again Steve had to know he was hurting Rachel—and apparently didn't care that he was.

That was one of the hardest things for her about this terrible day—and the terrible evening and night it would drift into. Rachel could picture Alice and Steve saying good-bye to the last wedding guest, then going upstairs together hand in hand. She wished more than ever she hadn't insisted on living in that house with Steve, sharing the bedroom he had shared with Alice. It was all too easy to picture them there, having once been there herself.

And when it came time for Rachel to go to bed—alone—she tossed and turned, thinking of Steve and Alice in bed together.

Actually, as she had been more than once before, Rachel was wrong. At that particular moment Alice and Steve were not in bed together. They were still downstairs, sitting out on the terrace, wearing sweaters over their wedding clothes against the cool of the evening, in no hurry to go inside, savoring the sweetness of being alone together and of being back home.

They were sitting together on the glider, Steve with his feet stretched out in front of him, Alice curled up beside him. "I missed this place so much," she said. "It was like part of myself." She turned to smile at him. "Silly, isn't it?"

He shook his head. "No, not silly. I never should

have—" He broke off.

"Steven," she said, "one of the things that got us into trouble the last time was your feeling—and with reason, I admit—your feeling that I couldn't stand to hear even the sound of Rachel's name. Let's don't get into trouble that way again. Now, you were saying?"

He nodded and squeezed her knee. "I never should have lived here with Rachel. I agreed to it, I suppose, because I wanted to hurt you the way I felt you had hurt me."

Alice could tell from the pain in his voice how much it had cost him to say that. She reached for his hand and held it in hers. "It's all right, Steven. I understand."

In a minute he went on. "I know that was Rachel's reason. She wanted to hurt you, and no doubt about it." He shook his head again. "And the funny thing is, she never liked this house. Never. She didn't like the location, for one thing. She hated being out here all day by herself. Rachel likes being where the action is." He shook his head again. "But she was set on living here."

They rocked back and forth a few moments in silence. "I'm glad she didn't like it," Alice said. "If she had she would have left an imprint here—one that I would have had trouble getting free of. But I knew without your telling me that she didn't like it, because I don't feel her presence here at all."

"She felt yours," Steve said. "In spite of all her redecorating and changing things around. She felt you everywhere."

Alice smiled and squeezed his hand. "Well, the ghost is back and in the flesh, having chased all the bad spirits away."

He gave her hand an answering squeeze. "And I

couldn't be happier."

She shook her head and said in a doubtful tone of voice, "Couldn't you, Steven?"

He pulled her close. "I had forgotten how sometimes you can read me so well it's as if you were standing on the inside looking out." He sighed. "If only I didn't have to go away."

She tightened her grip on his arm. "Maybe you won't have to, darling."

"My love," he said, "you mustn't count on that. It will only make things worse for you when I do have to go."

"All right," she agreed. "But then let's don't think about it. Not until we have to. Not tonight, anyhow."

"No," he agreed. "Not tonight." He hugged her to him even more tightly. "Have I thanked you for today?"

She smiled at him. "I don't think so."

He kissed her—a gentle, sweet, loving kiss. "Thank you for marrying me, Alice. For being my wife."

"Oh, Steven, thank you for letting me. I love you so much."

"And I you."

She pulled back to look at him, then bent toward him. "Kiss me again, please."

He kissed her—a lover's kiss, starting with tenderness, changing quickly to mounting passion.

She broke away. "Oh, Steven," she said breathlessly. "Oh, darling."

They kissed again, and this time it was the kind of kissing and fondling that Rachel lay sleepless in bed imagining, Steven imploring, wanting, demanding; Alice offering, also wanting, also demanding. At length, unable to stem desire any longer, they broke apart, and, arm-in-arm, headed upstairs and into their bedroom, where they consummated their marriage.

Steve and Alice had a week of being alone together, and then Steven was called back into court and given a six-month prison term at the Berryville State Prison, a minimum-security facility about an hour's drive north of Bay City.

Alice wanted to drive him there, but he refused to let her do it. Standing in the open front doorway with her on that warm, sunny day, he said, "I want to think of you as I see you now—here in our house. Not at the gates of a prison."

Her cornflower blue eyes filled with tears.

"And smiling," he said. "Not crying."

She wiped the tears from her eyes and tried to smile.

"The radiant one," he said. "My Alice smile."

She tried her hardest, but she couldn't come up with it. She threw her arms about him. "Oh, darling, stay safe."

He held her close. "I will, darling, I will. Will you be all right here?"

"I'll be fine," she said. "It's you I'm worried about."

He pulled back to look down at her, trying to reassure her. "There's nothing to worry about. No, darling, I mean it. It's a minimum-security facility—not like a regular prison at all. It's like a big dorm. There's not a thing to worry about. And it's only for six months. It could have been much worse, Alice."

"Yes," she said, and swallowed with difficulty, "I know." She swallowed again. "And you'll come back to me, Steven?"

"Of course I will, my darling. There's nothing anybody can do to keep me from doing that." He drew her to him again, kissed her again. "I have to leave now, darling." Steve reluctantly turned away from her.

She nodded, then watched him get in his car and drive off, continuing to stand in the doorway even after she couldn't see him any longer.

A week and a half later she went to Berryville to visit him. They met in the visitor's lounge, a room not so different from the visitors' lounges at Bay City Memorial Hospital—linoleum on the floor, flowered draperies at the windows, molded plastic furniture in various colors. Knots of people sat around the room, talking, drinking vending-machine coffee and sodas, some smoking, more not.

Steven looked better than when he had left her ten days ago. She already knew how he spent his days. He had written to tell her that he worked in the fields of the prison farm, and he had a tan to prove it.

"I gave them a surprise," he told Alice after they embraced one another. "They didn't think I knew anything about farming." Steven had grown up on a farm.

"Then it's not too bad?" she asked.

"No," he said, shaking his head. "It's not bad at all. Everything is locked into a routine, and everything is done to bells and whistles, but you get used to that. Or at least I suppose I will in time." He took her hand in his and searched her face. "But it's you I want to hear about. Are you okay?"

"Yes, Steven, I'm fine."

He continued to search her face. "You say that, but you don't sound it. And you don't look it. You've lost some weight. Aren't you eating?"

She sighed. "Yes, but not very well, I guess."

He frowned. "Why not?"

"Oh, I don't know. I don't seem to get hungry."

What she was saying alarmed him. "Alice. Darling." He squeezed her hand in his. "What's the trouble? What aren't you telling me?"

She glanced around at the other visiting couples. Some were more than couples. Some were family groups, with small children clinging to their mothers— or to their fathers.

She returned her attention to her own husband. "It's nothing, Steven. Really. There isn't anything the matter with me. It's just . . ."

His frown deepened. "Just what?" He followed her second glance around the lounge. "Darling, are you worried about me? Is that it?"

She shook her head. "Not worried exactly. I just—I just can't get used to the idea of your being here. Locked up, I mean. Not free to come and go or do what you want. Oh, Steven, isn't it awful for you?"

He pulled her to him, holding her close, trying to come up with the right words to reassure her. "Sweetheart, it isn't that bad. Honest. I miss you, of course. I miss you dreadfully. I count the days until I see you. But the work makes it bearable. When I'm out in the field I don't think about anything except the work I'm doing." He gave her a wry smile. "And much as I thought I hated my childhood, I find it exhilerating to be farming again, to work with the soil." He smiled. "I never appreciated the title of that Pearl Buck novel until these past ten days. *The Good Earth*. Now I know exactly what she was getting at."

"Do you?" Alice said. She too smiled, but it was far from being her radiant Alice smile.

"Darling," he said, pulling her to him again. "I'm fine. Honest I am. You're not to worry about me. Hear?"

She nodded. "Yes, darling, I hear you."

Still, when it came time for her to leave, her face was a mixture of sadness and relief.

After they parted, Steve went back to his dormitory. He had been there only a few minutes when a prison guard came into his room, saying, "Your wife is here to see you."

"But she just—" Steve broke off. Alice must have forgotten to tell him something, and he welcomed the chance to tell her another time he loved her and not to worry. He almost ran down to the lounge.

But instead of Alice, Rachel was standing there.

Chapter Nine

Rachel's Revenge

Steve's pleasure gave way to distaste. "What are you doing here?" he asked coldly.

Rachel smiled a little too sweetly. "I came to visit you, Steve. Aren't you glad to see me?"

"Not particularly, no. And why did you tell the guard you were my wife?"

She lifted her chin in the old, familiar gesture of defiance. "Legally I still am."

Steve rolled his eyes heavenward. "Rachel, that's hogwash."

"Is it?" she demanded. "When you got your divorce from me on false evidence?"

"Some of the evidence may have been false, but all of it certainly wasn't."

Rachel tossed her dark head. "So you say."

Steve hadn't asked Rachel to sit down, and he didn't now. He was not interested in encouraging a lengthy visit. "So the *judge* said," he answered her, "when he let the divorce become final. As I'm sure Sam has already told you."

She sniffed. "You and Sam don't know everything."

It was pointless arguing with her. All he wanted her to do was leave. "Look, Rachel," he said, "there are a lot of things I have put up with in this prison, but—"

"If you had stayed with me," she said, cutting him off, "you wouldn't be in this prison."

"I would rather be in this prison," he said, "than have stayed with you. Now, as I was saying, there are a lot of things I have to put up with here, but you're not one of them, so if you've said everything you came to say . . ."

"I haven't."

"Then say it."

She waved a hand at a conversational grouping of two molded plastic chairs and a molded plastic love seat—one of the few such groupings in the lounge that was not occupied. "Aren't you at least going to ask me to sit down?"

He let out a sigh. "All right, Rachel. Sit down." She sat on the love seat. He sat in one of the chairs. "Now," he said, "what's on your mind?"

She shrugged. "I want to know how you are."

"You can see how I am."

Color suffused her face. "You don't have to be mean to me, Steve."

"I didn't ask you to come here, Rachel."

She opened the clasp on her pocketbook, then closed it. "I don't know why you insist on denying you have any feeling for me."

He shook his head in amazement. "Rachel, that's something else I'm not going to get into with you. You have a way of twisting things I say to your advantage. If you really want to have a conversation with me, then let's talk about Jamie. Tell me how he is."

"Jamie's fine."

"Good. I'm glad to hear that. I'd like to see him."

Rachel stared at him, wide-eyed. "Here? In this prison?"

He waved an arm about him. "Other men's children come here to visit them. Look over there." He pointed to a corner of the lounge where a man was seated with his wife and two children, one of them about Jamie's age.

She did not so much as turn her head. "Well, Jamie's not going to. I can promise you that."

"Six months is a long time not to see him."

Rachel sniffed again. "You should have thought of that when you paid my father to lie for you. And speaking of that . . ." Opening her purse again, she took out a newspaper clipping and handed it to him. "I brought you this in case you haven't seen it."

The clipping was from a Bay City newspaper, repeating that Gerald Davis had pleaded guilty to a charge of perjury and had been sentenced to six months in prison. Steve handed the clipping back to her.

"You see what you've brought him to?" Rachel said, taking the clipping back and putting it in her purse.

"He didn't have to take the money," Steve said. "I didn't force it on him."

She gave him a nasty look. "That's easy for you to say."

Again he rolled his eyes heavenward. "Come on, Rachel. Next thing you'll be telling me I don't know what it means to be poor."

She flushed again. "Steve, please. I didn't come here to fight with you."

He shook his head again. "I'm still trying to figure out why you *did* come. To tell me about your father?"

"No. To tell you I saw Alice the other day and—"

She got no further. He was on his feet, frowning down at her, his face menacing. "You stay away from Alice, do you hear me?" he shouted.

Rachel gave him an injured look. "I haven't done anything to her."

He hadn't moved—or taken his eyes from her face. "I said stay away from her. And I mean exactly that, Rachel."

Rachel made a pretense of indifference. "All right. Then you can tell her for me."

"Tell her what?"

"That I want the house back."

Steve couldn't believe his ears. "Are you out of your mind?"

She glared at him. "I have a right to that house, and I want it."

"You have no right to it. None at all."

Up went the chin again. "It's half mine."

Again Steve shook his head. He couldn't imagine what had gotten into her—or rather, what she was up to. "Rachel, it's no such thing. What trick are you up to now?"

She gave him a sullen look. "I don't know what you're talking about."

Trying to get to the bottom of anything with her was like grappling with a slippery eel. He frowned down at her. "Why this sudden desire to have the house back? You never liked living in that house, even when I was living there with you."

"I'm not thinking of myself."

He snorted. "Not likely."

The chin went up a little higher. "Well, it's true, whether you want to believe it or not. It's for Jamie's sake. He misses the house. He misses the tree house you built there for him, and he misses the brook."

"Yes, I suppose he does," Steve admitted, "and I'm sorry about that. But Jamie can still get enjoyment out of those things when he comes to visit me there."

Rachel gave him a fierce and bitter look. "Jamie is not ever going to visit you there—not while Alice is in that house."

Steve pointed a finger at her. "If you think you can use Jamie to blackmail me, Rachel, you're wrong. We'll see what the judge has to say about where and when and how Jamie can visit me. That will be one of the first things I'll take up when I get out of here."

Picking up her purse, Rachel stood. "It won't have to wait that long, because I'm going to take it up with the judge myself."

Steve frowned at her in disbelief. "My visitation rights with Jamie?"

"No. The house. If you won't give it back to me, Steve, then I'll go to court to get it back."

In spite of himself he burst out laughing. "You do that, Rachel. You just do that. And lots of luck." Then he turned and walked out of the lounge, leaving her standing there.

Rachel's visit had come as a surprise to Steve, though thinking about it afterward he supposed he should have expected it. A greater surprise awaited him a few weeks later, when Ada walked into the visitors' lounge with Jamie at her side. Steve stared in disbelief at the pair of them, and once Jamie caught sight of Steve coming toward them across the crowded lounge, the boy didn't once take his eyes off his father.

"Rachel doesn't know I'm doing this," Ada said by way of greeting, helping Jamie off with his bright red nylon jacket. "And I've asked Jamie not to say anything to her, isn't that right, Jamie?"

He nodded, his eyes still on Steve.

Steve bent down to him, smiling. "Hello, son."

Instead of answering with a hello of his own, Jamie said, "I asked Grandma to bring me here to see you."

"That's right," Ada said, sitting down in one of the plastic chairs. "He did. That's why I did it."

"You couldn't have brought me anything better," Steve said, still drinking his fill of his seven-year-old son. He shook his head. "You've grown a mile, Jamie."

Jamie grinned. "An inch and a half."

"Well, it seems like a mile. Are you still playing Little League?"

Jamie nodded his head vigorously. "Yep. Still catching, too. Remember what you told me about catchers?"

Steve smiled again. "Sure I do."

Ada smiled too. "Jamie must have repeated that to me a dozen times or more. Good catchers are hard to come by."

"That's right," Steve said. "They are."

To his further surprise, Jamie hugged him—a tight hug—and when Steve hugged him back, the little boy's dark eyes filled with tears. "Oh, Daddy," he said, "I love you."

Steve's eyes now filled with tears. "Oh, son," he said, "and I love you. I love you, and I've missed you."

"Me too," Jamie said, clinging to his father.

Ada was also teary-eyed. Turning to Steve, she said, "Now you see why I had to bring him to you? I know you have your side and Rachel has hers about what's going on between you. But I couldn't see making Jamie go on suffering for that."

Steve picked Jamie up in his arms and sat with him on

his lap in the chair next to Ada's. "Ada," he said, "I don't know how I can ever repay you for this."

Ada shook her head. "You don't owe me anything, Steve. It's worth it just to see the two of you together."

"Daddy," Jamie said, playing with his father's hands, "is it awful staying here?" the young boy questioned.

Before answering him, Steve looked at Ada. She shrugged and said, "I told him where you were and why—in very general terms."

"I see," he said. He looked at his son. "No, Jamie, it's not awful." He hugged the little boy to him. "It's not somewhere I'd ever like to see you be, and I don't like having you see me here, but I did something wrong, and I have to pay for doing it, and this is how I'm paying for it."

Jamie frowned up at him. "With money, you mean?"

Steve shook his head. "No. Not with money. By staying here and working on the prison farm." He smiled. "That part of it I'm even enjoying. I'd forgotten how much I liked farming. Come here, son. Let me show you." He took Jamie to a window looking out on some of the fields and told him what each one was planted with. Then, as they went back to where Ada was seated, he said, "Maybe sometime when you come up here again, I can take you out to the fields. And the barns. To see the horses and cattle and the chickens and pigs. We've got them all."

"Well," said a man's voice behind them, "what do you know?"

Steve recognized the voice even before he turned. Standing behind him was Gerald Davis.

"Well," Gerald said, bending down to Jamie. "You remember your grandpa, don't you?"

Jamie frowned as if he wasn't sure. "I guess so."

"Of course you do," Gerald said. He turned to his former wife. "Hello, Ada. I didn't expect to see you here."

"I might say the same," she answered. She turned to Steve. "Well, I guess Jamie and I had better be going."

Gerald gave her a pained look. "Before I even get a chance to say two words to him?"

"He's had a big enough day already. Come here, Jamie. Let me put your jacket on you."

His jacket on, Jamie gave Steve a hug and a kiss.

"And your grandfather too?" Gerald asked.

"Sure, Grandpa." Jamie hugged him and kissed him.

When Ada and Jamie left, Steve walked to a window to watch them leave the prison. Gerald stood behind him. The older man said to Steve's back, "I've been waiting for this."

When Ada and Jamie had disappeared from view, Steve turned to Gerald. "Waiting for what?"

The pleasant face Gerald had turned to his grandson now had a nasty look on it. "The chance to tell you what I think of you. Turning me in wasn't part of our deal."

Steve gave him look for look. "Neither was opening your mouth. I didn't turn you in, Gerald. John Randolph did. After you blabbed to him. If you'd kept your mouth shut, as we both agreed to do, neither of us would be here."

"How was I to know you hadn't told your lawyer about our agreement?"

Steve shrugged. "If you haven't managed to come up with the answer to that in all the time you've had to think about it, my telling you isn't going to do any good."

Gerald looked at him sourly. "Always the wise guy."

"Oh, sure," Steve said. "That's why you see me where you do." He waved a hand around the lounge. "Because I know all the answers."

"It's easy for you to talk," Gerald said bitterly. "When you get out of here you'll still have your business to go back to. I had to sell mine."

"I'm sorry," Steve said, trying to sound sorry.

"Oh, yeah. I'm sure you are."

The last thing Steve wanted was trouble. "Look, Gerald," he said, "if you want to take out your frustrations on something, go down the hall to the gym. There are all kinds of things there to work out on. But spare me. I've got my own problems."

Gerald gave him another bitter look. "You never did have time for me, Steve. I was always a bum to you."

Steve spread his hands. "I never said that."

"You didn't have to. You made it plain enough the way you acted to me. Well, maybe things will be different here at Berryville. Here you're no better than I am."

Steve probably should have said nothing to that. But in his own way he was as frustrated as Rachel's father. "If that thought pleases you, Gerald, by all means hang on to it. Now if we've finished our conversation . . ."

Steve turned to go, but Gerald grabbed his arm, saying, "I haven't finished."

Steve tamped down the urge to strike the older man. "Take your hand off me," he said. When Gerald did, he said, "That's better. Now. You had something you wanted to say?"

Gerald glared at him. "That's right. I want you to know, Steve, I can make things rough here for you."

Steve shook his head. "Come on, Gerald. This isn't some grade-B movie."

The glare remained. "You just remember what I said."

Steve's answer was to turn and walk out of the lounge.

When Rachel learned that her father had been sent to Berryville, she went to see him. The visitors' lounge was crowded as always, and more people were smoking today. Nor did her father seem pleased to see her.

Rachel looked around her in distaste. "Isn't there somewhere more private than this?"

He shrugged. "There are a couple of lounges down the hall, but they might be crowded too."

One of the rooms he led her to had only one other couple in it, and they were sitting far enough away to allow Rachel and her father some privacy. "This is better," Rachel said. "Come sit here." She and her father sat down on two chairs, facing one another.

"How are you, Rachel?" he asked.

She sniffed. "As if you cared."

He stared at her in disbelief. "Did you come all the way up here to pick up where you left off in the courtroom? Because if that's what this is all about, I've got better things to do."

He would have gotten up, but Rachel put her hand out. "All right. I'm sorry. Maybe you do care about me. Only . . ." She straightened her shoulders, then let them slump. "Maybe you're right. Maybe I shouldn't have come here. I still can't get over—oh, well." She managed a smile of sorts. "It's too late for that, isn't it?"

Her father was looking at her warily. "Yes, it is."

"It's just that I—" She tried straightening her shoulders again. "Daddy, could you maybe make it up to me? Some, anyhow?"

He frowned at her. "How?"

This time she didn't hesitate. "I want Steve back."

Her father stared at her in dismay. "You're crazy."

She glared at him. "What's crazy about it? I had him once."

"Yeah. And lost him. Come on, Rachel. Sometimes a thing is worth fighting for, and sometimes it's not. And this is one of those times. Forget Steve Frame. Find somebody else."

"No," she said. "Never."

Gerald shook his head. This daughter of his was unbelievable. "Look," he said. "You're young. You're attractive. There must be any number of guys you could have if you wanted them. Why waste your time on a lost cause?"

Her chin went up. "He isn't a lost cause."

He shook his head again. "You're a hard one to argue with—and always have been. So all right, he isn't a lost cause. Not to you. He is where I'm concerned."

"Meaning you won't help me?"

"Meaning I can't. I can't get Steve Frame to give me the time of day."

"Why not?"

Gerald stared at her again. "Rachel, what do you mean, why not? I've never been able to get Steve Frame to give me the time of day. Or almost never. And things aren't any better here. If anything, they're worse. The day Jamie was here he—"

Rachel cut him off, the dismay on *her* face now. "Jamie was here?"

"Well, yeah."

Her voice rose in shock. "Jamie was here? Here? In this prison?"

"In the visitors' lounge, yeah. You mean you didn't know about it?"

"No, I did not. When was he here?"

"I don't know. A week or so ago."

"Who was he here with?"

Gerald was already sorry he'd mentioned it. "Your mother. She brought him here to see Steve."

Rachel clenched and unclenched her hands. She was furious. "And I specifically told Steve that Jamie was not to be brought here to see him. I don't want Jamie in a place like this."

Trying to placate her, Gerald said, "Maybe it wasn't his idea. Maybe it was your mother's."

Rachel nodded. "It probably was. Half of it, anyhow. And I'll see about that too. But first I'll take care of things at this end." She got to her feet. "Come on."

He frowned. "Where are you going?"

"To find Steve."

Reluctantly, Gerald stood up too. "He may be outside somewhere."

"There are only so many places he can be," she answered him. "This isn't Freedom Hall. Let's look in the main lounge first."

The other couple in the room had also decided to leave. Rachel and her father stepped back to let them leave first; then, before they could move forward, in walked Steve and Alice.

"Well," Rachel said, "speak of the devil."

Alice turned to her. "That's one of the things I've always liked most about you, Rachel. Your originality."

Rachel paid no attention. She was glaring at Steve. "I thought I told you I didn't want Jamie brought here to this prison. And don't bother asking me how I found out."

Steve didn't have to ask. He could guess. Not that it mattered. "Jamie wanted to come," he said. "He

152

asked to come. So your mother brought him."

"I don't believe you."

"It happens to be true, Rachel. Furthermore, Jamie and I patched up our differences. We're good friends again."

"Why didn't I hear anything about this?"

Steve sighed. "Because your mother and I figured you'd react exactly the way you are reacting—storming and screaming and carrying on. And who needs that?"

Rachel was even more exercised than she had been before he spoke. "All right," she said, "you and Mom put one over on me, and I suppose you think you can do it again. Well, I'm telling you right now you can't."

Exchanging a glance with Alice, Steve said as peaceably as he could, "Rachel, Jamie and I met in the visitors' lounge. We stayed in the visitors' lounge. The only part of the prison he saw other than that room was some farmland I showed him out the window. Now, I appreciate how you feel about a little boy like Jamie coming to a place like this. I honestly do. But I think the visit we had was more than worth it."

He could have saved his breath. Rachel wasn't buying any of it. "I don't care what you think," she snapped at him. "Jamie is my son, and I will not have him in this place again."

"He's my son too." Steve shook his head. "You know, Rachel, you have a strange way of talking about Jamie. There have been times when you've gone out of your way—and I mean *way* out of your way—to point out to me that Jamie is my son. Other times—like this one—you'd think he was no relation to me at all."

Rachel had the grace to flush, but that was all. Still glaring at Steve, she said, "I'm simply telling you what *is* going to be and what *isn't* going to be, at least as far as Jamie and this prison are concerned. And if you don't like it, then you don't like it, and I don't happen to care. You say the visit was worth it. Was it worth having Jamie lie to me about where he'd been that day?"

Gerald spoke up. "Now wait a minute, honey. If you didn't even know what day it was Jamie was here—and you didn't—how could he have lied to you about where he'd been?"

Rachel snapped at him, "You stay out of this."

Alice also spoke up. Putting a hand on Steve's arm, she said, "Darling, I'll speak to the judge about it for you. Maybe we can—"

Now Rachel snapped at her, cutting her off. "You'll do what? Alice, you stay out of this or I'll . . . I'll . . ."

Alice regarded Rachel steadily, calmly. "Yes, Rachel? You'll what?"

Rachel raised her chin. "Jamie is none of your business. He's Steve's and mine."

"Whatever is my business," Steve put in, "is Alice's as well. And that includes Jamie, Rachel, whether you like it or not." He turned to Alice. "Yes, do speak to the judge about it. See if we can get a ruling. Or maybe he'll be willing to talk to me." Taking Alice's hand, he turned back to Rachel. "And now if you'll excuse us, Rachel." He and Alice walked stiffly out of the room.

Rachel stood staring after them, furious, the color still high in her face. She made a fist and shook it at Steve's departing back. "How do you like that?" Making a face, she mimicked him, "'And now if you'll excuse us, Rachel.' Ohhh," she said, shaking the fist again, "sometimes I could kill him."

Her father shook his head sadly. "And only a few minutes ago you wanted him back. Come on. Let's get out of here ourselves. Visiting time is about up anyhow."

Together they walked down the hall toward the visitors' lounge. "I'm glad you came to see me, Rachel," her father said.

"Are you?" she asked, looking up at him.

"Sure I am. I didn't like being on the outs with you. I didn't like doing what I did to you, for that matter."

Rachel gave a quick little shake of her dark head. "Let's not get into that. It'll only get me more upset than I already am." She shook her fist again. "If you only knew how I hate Alice. How I've always hated her. So cool. So smart. So superior. I can't bear it."

Her father gave her a conciliatory look. "Honey, why get yourself in an uproar? Forget Steve, and Alice too. They're not wasting their time on you. Why should you waste your time on them?"

"I'd just like to show him, that's all."

"Why don't you let me show him for you?"

Rachel frowned. "How could you do that?"

He shrugged. "Oh, I could turn the screws a little. Here and there. Show him he's not the top banana he thinks he is."

Rachel's frown deepened. "You don't mean hurt him?"

Her father shrugged again. "I mean make his time here a little rougher on him than he expects, that's all."

They had been halfway to the visitors' lounge when Gerald made his offer. By the time they reached the door, Rachel's mind was made up. "All right. Do whatever you want to, then."

Chapter Ten
Monkey Business

Steve Frame had always been an intensely private person, for all his wheeling and dealing in the corporate world. At Berryville State Prison he did what he was asked to do by the prison authorities and, except when he was assigned to work with another prisoner, mostly stayed aloof from his fellow inmates.

Nobody took offense at this—or if anybody did, he kept it to himself. Until Gerald Davis went to work on them.

Because Berryville was a minimum-security facility, Steve soon found that he could meet with members of his business staff outside the regular visiting hours. This he welcomed because it meant he could retain an active hand in Steven Frame Enterprises. But it was this privilege that Gerald began turning to his advantage, and against Steve's.

He began spreading the story that Steve's business conferences were more in the order of monkey business—that the men who were brought to the prison to meet with him were not men at all but call girls.

"How is that possible?" a dishwasher asked Gerald when handed that in the kitchen as they stood at the sink together, washing and drying dishes.

"Have you ever seen any of those visitors Steve gets—the so-called business visitors?"

The dishwasher shook his head. "No."

"Well, I have," Gerald said. "And you can take it from me they're what I said they are. Call girls." He held out his hand. "Here, give me that platter."

Gerald counted on the dishwasher and a few other inmates to spread his lies to others, and, frustrated and unhappy, full of self-pity and envy, they did. Adding fuel to the flames was Gerald's contention that Steve was paying some official in the prison to do these favors for him, not needing to point out that, while the prisoners were incarcerated for their crimes, one or more of the men who kept them in there were committing crimes too—without having to be imprisoned for them.

At the same time Gerald began taunting Steve himself about his lady friends who came to see him, and wasn't it nice he had so much money he could pay for this privilege without having to think twice about it?

Had Steve really been thinking about Gerald and what he was saying, he might have guessed what Rachel's father was up to, but he didn't know Gerald was poisoning all those other minds against him, and he brushed aside Gerald's taunts as so nonsensical they weren't worth listening to.

Gerald's campaign to take Steve down a notch or two came to an unexpected climax on a hot afternoon in the middle of June when a work detail headed by Steve was unloading a truckload of fertilizer. Gerald was part of the work detail, and he stepped up his campaign, refusing to follow Steve's orders, taunting him some more about his mysterious visitors—his call girls.

Finally Steve had had it. He lashed out at Gerald, striking him. Losing his balance, Gerald fell off the truck and struck his head on its tailgate, knocking himself unconscious. Alarmed, Steve sent for help, then listened in shock and dismay as two other men on the work detail claimed that it was the blow from Steve that had knocked Gerald out. They repeated that story to the warden, and in the end Steve was transferred from Berryville to Manderville State Prison, a maximum-security facility.

If Berryville had made Alice uncomfortable, Manderville truly frightened her. Steve's new attorney went with her the first time she visited him there, but after a brief greeting he stepped aside so they could be alone together.

"Darling," Steve said, taking Alice in his arms, then holding her away from him so he could look at her, "are you all right?"

She nodded. "Yes, Steven, I'm all right," but she looked far from all right. She was thinner than before, and her face was totally without color.

Steve pulled her to him again. "Oh, God, how I've missed you."

She burst into tears and clung to him. "Oh, Steven, I can't bear to see you here."

"It's all right, Alice," he said, trying to soothe her. "Darling, it's only for a little while. Please. You mustn't take on this way."

She shook her head. "When I heard what they'd done to you, I was afraid I'd never see you again."

"That doesn't make sense."

"I know it doesn't, but that's how I felt all the same."

She clung to him again. "Oh, Steven, how did we ever come to this?"

He held her close. "Don't think about it. Just be thankful Gerald Davis recovered." Steve had been told that if Gerald died he would be charged with manslaughter.

Alice shook her head again. "It was my fault he fought with you, wasn't it?"

Steve stared at her in dismay. "Alice, it had nothing to do with you. He had a grudge against me, that's all. He resented the special privileges I was given."

"But," she persisted, "it was because of me that you paid him to testify for you. And because of me, he ended up in prison with you."

Steve shook his head. "No. It was all my doing. It was what I wanted. Alice, look at me." He put a finger under her chin and raised her face to his. "You mustn't blame yourself for anything that's happened. Darling, we've been through all of this before. None of this is your fault. None of it. And I won't have you thinking that way." He looked at her anxiously. "Will you promise me you won't?"

She answered his question with one of her own. "Steven, when will you get out?"

"I don't know. Soon, I hope." In his arms she shivered, and he gave her another anxious look. "Darling, what is it?"

"Nothing. It's just—I get so frightened that things will get worse instead of better."

"Alice, they can't."

She gave him such a sad look it tore at his heart. "We thought that before. And they have. Oh, Steven. It was so hard for me before—when you were at Berryville. But this. I can hardly bear the thought of this."

He pulled her to him again, again held her close. "Alice. Darling. Don't think about it. Put it out of your mind."

Again the sad look that tore at him. "I can't do that. Steven, if I don't have you—even to think about—I have nothing."

"Then think of me being at home with you."

"I've tried that, but it doesn't work."

From his corner of the room Steve's new attorney made his presence known. "I'm afraid our time's about up."

Steve took Alice in his arms and kissed her. "Think of how I love you, darling. Nothing will ever change that."

"Or my love for you," she said, her voice choked with tears. She clung to him, then pulled herself away, the tears running down her face. "Don't say good-bye, Steven. Please."

"All right." He lifted his hand in farewell, then watched her leave, full of concern for her, wishing desperately he could be free.

Sam Lucas had returned to John Randolph's law firm, and it was there that Rachel went to see him to pursue her demand that the country house be returned to her. Sitting down in a chair opposite his desk, she told him why she was there.

"Are you crazy?" Sam said, looking up from the papers he'd been studying, taking off his green eye shade. "You don't stand a chance of getting that house back."

"I don't see why not," she said.

"Well, for starters, because it never belonged to you."

"It belonged to me when I was married to Steve."

"No, Rachel, it didn't." Sam shook his head. "When

Alice divorced Steve she deeded the house to him. But it was never part of the property he shared with you. That was made very clear in the deed."

Rachel frowned at him. "But I lived there with him."

Sam picked up a pencil from his desk and rolled it back and forth between his hands. "His sister lived there with him too. Would you say she had any claim on owning it?"

Rachel tossed her head. "That's different."

"Yeah, well . . ." Sam silently rolled the pencil some more. "Forget about the house."

She gave him a hard look. "No, I won't forget about it. I want you to get it back for me."

"Rachel, I just explained it to you. There's no way I can."

"You can take it to court, can't you?"

He shook his head again. "Not without some kind of claim—and some kind of evidence to back up that claim. We don't have either one, claim or evidence." He sighed. "Rachel, you're wasting my time as well as your own. Forget about the house. You want more money out of Steve? That I can try for. I don't expect I'll get it, but at least I can try."

"No, I don't want any more money."

"That's refreshing."

"I want the house."

Sam sighed again. "It seems to me, if I remember clearly, there was a time when you came clamoring to me about wanting an apartment in town because you hated that house."

She raised her chin. "That was different."

"Rachel, that's your answer for everything. Now I've got work to do." He put his eye shade back on. "You can see yourself out, can't you?" He went back to his reading, pointedly ignoring her.

Rachel got up and stood there fuming for a moment before storming out of his office. Then she drove out to the house to confront Alice. She let herself in the front door and eventually found Alice in the master bedroom upstairs. "May I come in?" she asked.

The door was closed, and at first Alice told Rachel to go away, but when Rachel insisted on seeing her, claiming she had a message for her from Steve, Alice finally relented and opened the door to her. "What is it, Rachel?"

Surprised at how ghostly Alice looked, Rachel smiled her little self-deprecating smile. "Well, my goodness, Alice, are we just going to stand here talking in the doorway? You make me feel like a door-to-door salesman."

Alice opened the door wider. "Come in then." She went over and sat on the side of the king-size bed and waved Rachel to a blue velvet slipper chair. "What message do you have for me from Steven, Rachel? Have you been to see him at Manderville?"

"No. He gave me the message while he was still at Berryville."

Alice frowned. "I don't understand. What message would Steven give to you for me anyway? Why wouldn't he give it to me himself? Or to anybody else *but* you?"

Rachel smiled again. "You like to believe that Steve doesn't have any use for me, don't you, Alice? That's what you like to tell yourself."

"He *doesn't* have any use for you."

The smile turned sly. "Not any use, Alice? None at all? He fathered a son with me. He married me. He lived in this house with me. He slept in that bed with me.

And he did more than just sleep in it. I can guarantee you that."

"Rachel," Alice said, beginning to sound agitated, "I don't want to talk to you anymore. I want you to leave."

"In a few minutes, Alice. When I'm finished saying what I have to say."

"Then say it."

"All right," she said, nodding. "I came out here to tell you I'm moving back into the house."

Alice looked confused. "What house?"

"This one."

Now Alice stared at her. "This one? Are you mad?"

Rachel shook her head. "It's my house, Alice, and I want it back. And Steve wants me to have it back."

"I don't believe you."

"Well, I don't care what you believe, Alice. It's the truth. That was the message he gave me to give you— when I went to see him one time at Berryville."

"I don't believe you," Alice repeated. "He would have said something to me."

Rachel tossed her head. "He doesn't always tell you what goes on between him and me, whether about Jamie or about other things."

"Rachel, you lie!"

"Maybe about some things, yes. But I've never lied to you about Steve—about what we have between us. Something you've never had with him."

Alice slid off the bed to her feet. "Rachel, get out of here."

She stayed where she was. "Who is the mother of Steve's child, Alice? His only child. Not you, me. Oh, I know Steve is very fond of you. Very devoted to you. Because of what you stand for. Things he admires and looks up to." She made a scornful face. "But that's not love, Alice. Not the kind of love Steve has for me."

Alice began looking around her, as if for something to throw at her tormentor. "Rachel, if you don't get out of here—"

Rachel calmly cut her off. "You're the one who has to go, Alice. Because that's the way Steve wants it. That's what he told me to tell you. He wants you out of here, do you understand that?" she persisted.

Alice finally found something to throw. She picked up a bedside lamp, jerked it out of its outlet, and hurled it at Rachel. It crashed and broke on the floor. Then Alice hurled herself at Rachel. Rachel dodged her and ran from the house, Alice still chasing her, screaming at her.

That evening Alice's brother, Russ, found her in a state of collapse, and the next day he drove her to a private sanitarium.

The following day, when Rachel went over to see her mother, she played the entire incident down. Her mother was in the kitchen, beginning dinner. In an indifferent manner, Rachel told her what she had done, then said, "I did it for Jamie. He misses living in that house, and he wants to be back there."

Ada shook her head. "Just because Jamie wants something doesn't mean he can have it. Especially when what you say he wants happens to be somebody else's property." Ada took a carrot out of the refrigerator and took it to the sink to scrape it. "I'm ashamed of you, Rachel. How could you do something as vicious as that to Alice?"

Rachel pretended not to understand. "I'm only trying to take back what belongs to me. I don't see what's vicious about that."

Ada turned from the sink. "That house doesn't

belong to you, and it never did." Rachel started to interrupt, but Ada put a hand up. "You're talking to me, Rachel. Your mother. I may not have as much education as some of the fancy friends you've been picking up lately, like Iris Carrington and her following, but I know what is and what isn't a fact. And the fact is, you have no claim on that house at all. And look what you've done to Alice in the process."

Rachel shrugged. "I didn't do anything to Alice except say what I went there to say."

"You put her in the hospital. She's had a collapse."

Rachel sniffed. "Just because Alice has had a collapse doesn't mean I caused her to have it. She was perfectly all right when I left her. A little exercised, maybe, but nothing more than that."

Secretly convinced that, by collapsing, Alice was simply demonstrating once again that she always buckled under pressure instead of standing up and fighting for what she wanted, Rachel hurried back to Berryville to take advantage of this favorable turn of events—under the guise, of course, that she was doing it for Jamie.

She made an appointment with the warden, asking him to drop the assault charges against Steve, saying her son—their son—needed his father.

"My dear young woman," the warden said, "in the first place, dropping the assault charges against Steven Frame isn't entirely up to me. And in the second place, even if the charges were dropped, that doesn't mean Mr. Frame would be discharged from prison."

From her chair in front of the warden's desk Rachel frowned at him. "But at least he could be brought back here from Manderville, couldn't he?"

"Yes."

"And that way Jamie could at least visit him," she said, conveniently forgetting her vow never to have Jamie come to Berryville again.

"The person for you to speak to," the warden said, "is your father."

The warden had Gerald brought to his office, explaining that Rachel wanted to see him, and that while the warden would remain in the room, he would stay out of the discussion.

At that Rachel turned to her father. "I came here," she said, "to ask that the charges against Steve be dropped."

Gerald stared at her wide-eyed. "Dropped? Why dropped? He tried to kill me."

Rachel shook her head. "That isn't what Steve says. He says he only hit you because you provoked him into doing it, and that you hit your head falling off the truck and that's what knocked you out."

"When did he tell you all that?"

"He didn't tell it to me. He told his lawyer. But that's not the point. The point is what he says happened."

Gerald looked from the warden to Rachel. "What Steve says happened isn't what the guys who saw it said."

She sighed. "Daddy, does it matter?"

He gave her a bitter look. "I almost got killed. Doesn't that matter?"

"Yes, of course it does, but you *didn't* get killed, and you're all right now, aren't you? Look. If you'll drop the charges against Steve he can come back here to Berryville, where he can have visitors."

Her father's face cleared. "So that's it. You want to see him."

"No. Jamie wants to see him."

"Jamie wanted to see him before when he was here, but you wouldn't hear of it."

Rachel flushed. "Well, I've changed my mind."

Gerald gave her a skeptical look. "Changed your mind, Rachel, or changed your tactics?"

Her color heightened. "That's not a fair thing to say. I didn't know before how much Jamie missed his father, or how much he still cared about him."

Gerald was unmoved. "If you didn't know it, Rachel, it's because you didn't choose to know it. You hear what you want to, you see what you want to, and you would sell your own grandmother if it suited your purposes. No, I'm not dropping the charges."

Very much aware of the warden's presence, Rachel gave her father a hard look. "Then maybe I should tell Steve to file countercharges, and I'll be his first witness. And you want to know what I'll say? I'll say—and I'll be telling the truth, unlike some people I know—I'll say that you told me you were going to make life rough for him here at Berryville. That you were going to turn the screws. Those were your very words. To show him he wasn't the top banana he thought he was."

"And who asked me to do that?"

Rachel lifted her chin. "I did not ask you to do anything to Steve. The only thing I asked you was not to hurt him."

Her father nodded. "Meaning you went along with what *you* say I was going to do. That makes you just as liable as I am, Rachel. Try putting that one on for size."

Rachel gave him another hard look, but she didn't say anything, and finally Gerald sighed and said, "All right. Have it your way." He turned to the warden. "As far as I'm concerned you can drop the charges."

Rachel was all smiles—and all ready to kiss and make

up—but Gerald asked permission of the warden to leave, which he did without so much as a glance in her direction.

Instead of being returned to Berryville, Steve was paroled. On his way to the sanitarium to see Alice, he stopped off at the house to confer with the caretaker who had been hired to look after the property until Steve could look after it himself. While he was there the front door opened, and in came Rachel with a suitcase. "Well," she said, smiling at Steve and the caretaker, setting the suitcase down in the foyer, "I didn't expect a welcoming committee. How are you, Steve?"

Steve couldn't believe his eyes. Looking from Rachel to the suitcase and back to her, he said, "What are you doing here, Rachel?"

"I'm getting ready to move in."

"You're what?"

"What I just said. I've ordered the moving van for tomorrow. I only brought a few things with—"

He cut her off. "If this is some game, Rachel, you can stop it right now."

Up went the chin. "It's not a game. I'm serious."

"Then you can stop it anyhow. You're not moving into this house."

The chin went higher. "I'd like to know who's going to stop me."

"You're looking at him." Steve turned to the caretaker. "I want the locks changed on all the doors. Until that happens I want you to stay here. Under no circumstances is this woman you see here—or anybody else who doesn't have my authorization—to be allowed inside the house. Is that clear?"

"Yes, sir," the caretaker said.

Steve nodded toward Rachel. "And now if you'll see her out, please."

"Yes, sir."

As the caretaker moved toward her, Rachel said, "You can't do this to me, Steve. This house is mine."

Steve didn't answer her but turned and walked into the living room.

In an hour's time he was on his way to Clareview, the private sanitarium. He had been warned by Alice's brother, Russ, that Alice might not see him, and in fact she wouldn't.

Steve met with her psychiatrist instead. The psychiatrist tried to explain to Steve what was going on. After they had discussed Alice's penchant for running away from problems, the psychiatrist said, "This time she is running away mentally, and I think I can tell you why. Now, I know you think that Rachel is the core of the problem, but she isn't." The psychiatrist put up a hand to forestall interruption. "I didn't say she isn't *part* of the problem. She is and very much so. But only symbolically."

Steve was frowning in confusion.

"But the reason Alice is running away is fear. She's afraid of losing what she wants. And one good way of avoiding that is never to possess it." He spread his hands. "What I mean to say is, if you don't have something, you can't very well lose it. Right?"

Steve nodded. "Yes."

"And if you can't bear losing something, if you are afraid that losing it will destroy you, then you protect yourself by denying yourself that something."

Steve was trying very hard to understand what the doctor was saying, but he couldn't. Shaking his head, he said, "But it doesn't make sense—I mean, if you're talking about me, about Alice and me. Doctor, I love Alice more than I have ever loved anybody or anything in this world."

"And yet she's lost you."

Steve shook his head again. "Because of the lies Rachel told her about the house? But Alice had to know they were lies. It makes no sense at all." Getting up from the chair he'd been sitting in, Steve began pacing back and forth. "Rachel. It's always Rachel. I had thought that finally Alice and I had that all straightened out. For good."

The doctor shook his head. "I'm not sure anything in anybody's life is ever straightened out for good. And when you add in the tremendous strain your wife has been under since you were sent to Berryville, the guilt she feels for her part in it . . ."

Steve stopped his pacing to turn to him. "But she had no part in it."

"Not from your point of view, no. But from hers, very much so." The doctor stood up. "I think, Mr. Frame, if you can just be patient and put your trust in me, we'll bring your wife around all right."

And for the time being Steve had to be satisfied with that.

He got a different kind of satisfaction a few days later. He was working in his office when his secretary buzzed him to say that Rachel was there to see him. "I tried to get her to leave," she said, "but she started making a scene."

"That's all right," Steve said. "I'll take care of it." After cradling the phone, he went to his door and opened it, jerked his head toward Rachel, held the door for her.

Smiling, she came in. "Hello, Steve."

He closed the door and went back to his desk and sat

behind it. "What do you want, Rachel?"

"My goodness," she said, sitting in a chair across from the desk, "you don't sound very friendly."

He gave her an impassive look. "I don't feel very friendly. Not after this latest stunt of yours."

"If you're talking about my wanting the house back—"

"I'm talking about your causing Alice's breakdown. I'm trying very hard, Rachel, not to think about it, but your coming here makes that almost impossible. Now would you like to know why I try so hard not to think about your causing Alice's breakdown?"

Rachel was no longer smiling. "All right. Why?"

He leaned across the desk toward her. "Because I could kill you, Rachel. And I mean that literally. I would like to put my hands around your neck and choke the life right out of you."

She shrank back in the chair.

"Now I suggest you get out of my sight and stay out of my sight."

Rachel got to her feet and backed a little away from him, but she wasn't finished with him. "You don't mean that, Steve. You can't. If it wasn't for me you wouldn't be sitting here in your office. You'd still be in jail. And that's the truth."

Steve had been speaking harshly to her, and his tone of voice didn't change. "What do you want me to do, Rachel? Thank you?"

"Well, my goodness, Steve," she said, a little tremulous, "it's true. I went to Berryville and got my father to drop the charges against you. And he didn't want to drop them, either. But I persuaded him to. And I persuaded the warden to also. You could at least show me a little gratitude."

"Get out, Rachel."

She backed away a little farther. "You're just upset, that's all, Steve. When you've had time to cool down a little you'll—"

He got to his feet and started around the desk toward her.

She put a hand up. "I'm going. I'm going. Don't you come near me." She turned and ran to the door, opened it, and ran out.

And still she wasn't finished with him.

Chapter Eleven
Love Prevails

The time came when Alice's psychiatrist decided she could return to her parents' home in Bay City, but on one condition—that she not secrete herself away in her room upstairs, refusing to see anybody or have anything to do with them. Explaining that to her parents, he said, "She would have to have some contact with the members of the family. I would have to insist on that."

Neither Jim nor Mary Matthews had any objection to this.

"And there's a further condition," the doctor continued. "One that goes without saying, really. That she continue her therapy with me."

Jim nodded. "We'll bring her here as often as you say."

"That won't be necessary. I have an office in Bay City."

"Oh, of course," Jim said. "I'd forgotten."

And so Alice went back to her parents' home. Her brother, Russ, told Steve about it, saying she still didn't want to see him, but he was sure the time would soon come when she would meet with him again.

Russ patted Steve's shoulder. "I know it's hard for you to hear this, Steve, but be patient. Wait. Hope."

Steve nodded. "I'll wait. Forever if it takes that long."

Steve left Russ in his office at the hospital and headed back to his own office, but on the way he stopped at a florist's shop, where he asked that a dozen American beauty roses be sent to Alice every day from then on, until he had the order canceled.

"Yes, sir," the florist said. "And what would you like the card to say?"

Steve shook his head. "No card. No card is necessary."

Just as Russ had been given the job of telling Steve that Alice had left the sanitarium to return to her parents' home, and that she still was obsessed with the matter of Rachel, so it was Russ who was given the job of delivering the next hard blow to Alice.

Thinking that maybe her problem was physical as well as emotional—she was still much too thin—he ordered a complete checkup for her. A few nights later he went to the house to see her. He found her sitting in the swing on the front porch.

"Where are the folks?" he asked, joining her there.

"Over at the Andersons'," Alice answered. "It's their bridge night."

He turned to frown at her. "Are you here all alone?"

"Yes." Alice put a hand on his knee. "I don't mind, Russ."

"I know you don't, but I do."

She shrugged. "It can't hurt anything for me to be alone sometimes, Russ. I'm not a child."

"No. I know that."

For a few minutes they swung back and forth in

silence. Then Alice said, "Why did you come to see me, Russ? And don't say you didn't have any reason."

"No. I won't say that. I have some bad news for you, Alice."

She sighed. "I thought so."

"I'm sorry."

"It doesn't matter. What is it, Russ? The bad news."

He couldn't see any point in prolonging things—or in trying to lead up to it slowly. Still he spoke as gently as he could. "You're not going to be able to have any more children, Alice."

Again they rocked back and forth in silence. It was a warm night. At last Alice said, "I've thought that was the case ever since I lost my baby—when the doctor said I had to wait a while, and then a while longer, and then longer still."

Russ nodded. "I'm sorry, Alice. It's rough news, I know."

"It would be rougher on Steven."

Russ frowned at her. "What do you mean, 'would be'?"

"If he knew."

His frown deepened. "Meaning he isn't going to?"

"Yes." She turned to him, clutching at his shirt sleeve. "Russ, promise me you won't tell him."

"If you don't want me to, then of course I won't."

"I don't want anybody to tell him. You or anybody else."

Russ patted her arm. "Medical information is confidential, Alice. You know that. Nobody will tell him. Nobody unauthorized will have access to the files. But do you think you're being fair not telling him? Don't you think he has a right to know?"

Alice's face had a set look to it. "Why? So he'll

have even more reason to feel sorry for me?"

"Alice," Russ said, "Steve doesn't feel sorry for you. He loves you. You know that," he assured her.

"No. He only thinks he does."

Russ patted her arm again. "Well, I'm not going to argue with you. I'll let your psychiatrist do that. And he'll have to know, of course. I can't withhold this information from him."

"I understand that. It's Steve I don't want to know."

Russ frowned at her again. "Why, Alice? Is it only because you think he'll feel sorry for you?"

"No. Because he wants to have more children. And he should have more. If I can't give them to him, somebody else can. Rachel can. She can, and she wants to."

"She may want to," Russ agreed, "but that's the last thing Steve wants. I can guarantee you that."

Whether or not Alice was right about Rachel wanting to give Steven more children was debatable. Rachel hated being pregnant. The only reason she hadn't minded being pregnant with Jamie was the hold it gave her over Steve. But as for her wanting Steven, there was no question about that. She wanted him, and she believed she could have him—if she could just persuade him that his true happiness lay with Jamie and herself, not in his hopeless pursuit of the unattainable Alice.

For some time after Steve threw her out of his office, she stayed away from him. Then she went there again to see him on the pretext that her October alimony check had not arrived.

He was not pleased to see her. After she had seated herself across from his desk and made her complaint, he said, "I've told you before, Rachel, that if that happens you're to check it out with my lawyer. He's the one who authorizes the payment. I have nothing to do with it."

She sniffed. "I don't like dealing with your lawyer."

"Tough."

She settled herself more comfortably in the chair. "And anyhow, I wanted to talk to you about something else."

"What?"

"The house."

Rachel's enemies as well as her friends had often observed that her greatest talent lay in destroying whatever she had managed to get for herself. Talk about Alice's house was the last thing Steve wanted to hear from her, and he set about saying so. "There's nothing to talk about where the house is concerned," he said gruffly. "And don't hand me that line about Jamie wanting to live there. Jamie and I had a little talk about that. I was trying to explain to him why he couldn't live there, and he said it didn't matter, it was a nice house, and he'd like to come visit me there, but he didn't care all that much about it. You were the one who did."

Color flooded into Rachel's face. "He was just trying to be nice about it."

Steve grunted. "Eight-year-old boys don't go out of their way to be nice about something. Not to their fathers. So for the last time, Rachel, forget the house. That house is for Alice. It always was, and it still is."

"Alice doesn't want that house any more than she wants you. She's made that clear enough."

Steve gave her a menacing look. "Rachel, I will not discuss Alice with you. Not now and not any time."

She tossed her head. "I was just making an observation."

"Well, you can keep your observations to yourself. Now, do you have any further business with me?"

"I want to know where you're taking Jamie this afternoon."

"I haven't decided. Anything else?"

She glared at him. "Now wait a minute, Steve. You can't brush me off like that. I have a right to know where you and Jamie go and what you do."

"If you ask him tonight in a very nice way I'm sure he'll tell you." Steve pushed back from his desk and stood up. "Anything else, Rachel? I have a very busy morning ahead of me."

She too stood up. "Oh, all right. I was leaving anyhow."

Rachel went from Steve's office to her mother's house, telling her mother where she'd just been.

Ada was sitting at her kitchen table looking through some cookbooks, and Rachel sat down with her. "What did you have to see Steve about?" Ada asked.

"Oh," Rachel said airily, "nothing really. He just enjoys having me stop by there every now and then."

"I bet," Ada said. "After what you did to Alice, I'm sure he's just crazy to have you come see him."

Rachel sniffed. "There's nothing wrong with Alice. At least not anymore. She's gone back to work at the hospital. Did you know that?"

Ada was surprised. "No, I didn't. When did that happen?"

"Oh, a week or so ago. I ran into Russ the other day. He told me."

Ada closed the cookbook she'd been looking through and opened up another one. "Well, I'm glad to hear it. Is she still not seeing Steve?"

Rachel smiled. "That's right. She's still not seeing

him. You wait, Mom. You'll see. You and everybody else."

For all the damage Rachel had done, Ada still hated to see her get hurt. She put a hand on Rachel's arm. "Rachel, honey, don't do this to yourself. You'll only end up hurt—and with everybody laughing at you."

"No, Mom," Rachel said, shaking her head, a determined look on her heart-shaped face, "no, I won't. I'm going to end up with Steve. That's how I'm going to end up."

And try as she might, Ada couldn't talk her out of that.

A couple of weeks later, on impulse, Steve got into his car and drove over to the Matthews house to see Alice. It was her day off from the hospital, and he wanted to talk to her. Or simply look at her. Convince himself she was still there.

Not surprisingly, the house was filled with red roses.

And Alice was there. She came to the door to meet him, opened it for him, asked him to come in. Then, once inside with the door closed again, they simply stood looking at each other.

"I hope you don't mind, Alice," he began, not taking his eyes from her face.

She hadn't taken her eyes from his face either. "No, Steven, it's all right." She shrugged—or maybe it was a shiver. "I mean, we couldn't go on the way we have been indefinitely, could we?"

"No."

For a few moments neither of them said anything; then Alice said, "Did you want to see me about something, Steven?"

"No," he said. "Yes." And before he knew what he

was saying, he said, "Alice, I love you." He almost wished he hadn't said it. The last thing he wanted to do was frighten her off, before he had a chance to say all the things that had been bottled up inside him.

She didn't run away from him, but she started trembling. "Steven . . .," she began.

He didn't let her get any further than that. "Alice," he said, "I'm sorry. There's so much more that I want to say to you, that I *have* to say to you. And yet, when you get right to it, that's what it all comes down to. That I love you. And I want you. I know you say you don't love me, but—"

This time it was she who cut him off. "No. I never said that."

He searched her face. "You mean you do love me?"

She didn't answer him right away, but at last she said, "Yes. I do love you."

He reached out to her, then let his hands fall to his sides. "Then what are we doing to each other, Alice? I love you. You love me. I want you. You want me. Why are we living the way we are—if you can call this living. Why don't you come home to me? Don't we both want that?" Again he reached out to her, and again let his hands fall to his sides. "Don't we?"

It took her even longer to answer him this time. "Steven," she said, starting to look upset, "it isn't just a—just a yes-no thing. There are so many complications."

"There aren't any," he objected, "except in your mind." He spread his hands in an appeal to her. "I don't know of any."

She frowned at him. "All the trouble I've brought to you? That doesn't count?"

"No. Absolutely not." He shook his head. "What

trouble was brought to me I brought on myself."

"You keep saying that."

"Alice, I keep saying it because it's true. And if that's all that's standing between us . . ."

She shook her head. "No, Steven, it isn't all."

"What then? What is it?"

She only shook her head again.

"Alice," he begged, "what?"

"Steven," she answered slowly, "you think I can give you everything you want, but I can't."

Again he searched her face. "Are you talking about happiness?"

"Yes. In a way."

"What do you mean, in a way?"

Tears came into her eyes. Brushing them away, she said in a mournful voice, "Steven, it's no use."

"Is something bothering you? Something I don't know about?"

"Steven," she repeated, "it's no use."

And that was all he could get out of her. And then she asked him to leave.

He went straight to the hospital, where he caught up with Russ in a fourth-floor corridor. He told him about meeting with Alice, of her admission that she loved him, and then he said, "Is something bothering her?"

Russ nodded. "Yes."

"What is it?"

"I can't tell you, Steve. I'm sorry, but I can't."

"Why not?"

"Because I promised her I wouldn't."

"Well, why did you do that?"

"Because she insisted. Look, Steve. I tried to persuade her to tell you, but you know how stubborn she can be."

Steve nodded. "Yes, I know that. But why didn't she want me to know?"

Russ shook his head. "I can't tell you that without in effect telling you what it is that's bothering her."

Frustrated, Steve said, "Can't you tell me anything?"

"I can tell you I think she's wrong—the same as I've already told her."

Suddenly alarmed, Steve reached out to his brother-in-law. "Russ, tell me it isn't—she doesn't have some terrible—"

Russ cut him off. "No. No, it's not that kind of problem."

"Well, then, what?"

"Steve, we're back where we started. The only thing I can suggest to you is that you appeal to her again. Maybe write to her about it. I know that sounds crazy when the two of you live so close. But, well—a letter is a powerful thing, something she can read and reread and think about and read again. I think it's what I'd do if I were in your place."

Steve went back to his office, deciding he would take Russ's advice. But it was a letter his whole future depended on, and he wanted to give it plenty of thought.

While he was still thinking, Rachel—as usual—took the matter out of everyone's hands.

Not feeling well, she made an appointment with her physician, expecting to have to wait, appointment or no. He was always running late.

The physician had a new nurse, who was also a newcomer to Bay City. When Rachel gave her name as Mrs. Frame, the nurse started riffling through her file, came to a folder marked, "Frame, Alice," and looked no further. She was putting it on her desk when her buzzer rang. She picked up the phone. "Yes, Doctor? . . . Yes. Certainly." She cradled the phone and went into the doctor's inner office.

Seeing the wrong folder, Rachel picked it up and began looking through it. She came to a lab report. Wide-eyed with surprise and excitement, she pocketed the report and put the folder back on the desk.

The nurse came back out. "The doctor will be a few more minutes," she said.

Rachel checked her watch. "Long enough for me to get a cup of coffee in the cafeteria?" The doctor's office was located on the ground floor of the hospital.

"Yes. Be back in fifteen minutes."

Rachel went not to the cafeteria but to a copying machine in the hospital gift shop. She copied the report, killed some time, then went back to the doctor's office.

The doctor, of course, noticed that the folder the nurse handed him was the wrong one. Rachel was terrified he would open it and see that the lab report was missing—she hadn't yet had the opportunity to replace it—but he didn't. He merely asked the nurse to bring him the correct folder.

It wasn't until after her examination was over that Rachel was able to return the report. Pretending she had lost her car keys in the dressing room, and knowing another patient was already undressing in there, she asked the nurse to look for the keys for her. While the nurse was out Rachel returned the report to Alice's folder, then, when the nurse returned, pretended to find her keys in her coat pocket.

Rachel, who had been diagnosed as having slightly elevated blood pressure, drove from the hospital to Steve's office, her hopes more than slightly elevated.

At first his secretary refused to even let Steve know she was there to see him, but when Rachel threatened to create a scene, just as she had threatened the last time, the secretary gave up and buzzed Steve to tell him.

He opened his inner office door. "What do you want, Rachel?"

"I have something to show you and something to tell you," she said.

"What?"

"Can't I talk to you in private, Steve? Please."

He sighed. "All right. Come in."

She went in and he closed the door behind her, then went to sit at his desk while she sat down in a chair in front of it.

"What do you have to show me?" he said.

She took the copy of the report out of her purse and handed it to him.

He took it from her and looked at it, frowning. "Where did you get this?"

She shrugged, prepared to lie as always. "The nurse in the doctor's office gave it to me by accident. I didn't even know what it was until I got home and looked at it. But when I did, I thought you would be interested in it, so I made a copy for you."

Steve shook his head. "So this is what's been bothering her." To make sure, he checked the date on the report, then said, "It has to be." For the first time in a long time he had reason to be grateful to Rachel, and he smiled at her. "I can't tell you how much this means to me, Rachel—or how I'll ever be able to thank you."

Sure now that her gambit had paid off, Rachel smiled back at him. "I did it because I love you, Steve—the same reason I do everything I do. Because I love you. Because we belong together."

He stared at her in horror. "Rachel—"

She cut him off. "No. Don't say anything until you hear me out. Please. Steve, I know you think you don't like me. You think it's Alice you love, Alice you have to have. Alice who makes your life complete. But it's me, Steve. Me you need to make your life complete." Triumph was shining on her face, shining in her eyes. "We're the same kind of people, Steve, you and me. We're fighters, we're tough, we bounce back. And we don't give up, Steve." She spread her hands out in a gesture of appeal. "Steve, we've had some great times together. Not even you can deny that."

"No," he said, "but—"

Again she wouldn't let him go on. "You don't have to explain to me, Steve. You don't have to apologize or try to make me understand. I do understand, don't you see? Because I *am* so much like you. Steve, take me back. Please. We have Jamie. We can have other children. We can be a real family—the way we were before."

"Rachel," Steve said with a stab of pity, "don't do this to yourself."

But she wouldn't listen to him. And when he tried to explain that it was only Alice he loved, only Alice he wanted, she wouldn't believe him. She left his office convinced he would come back to her as soon as Alice had released him.

Rachel had no sooner left his office than Steve left it as well, going to the Matthews house. Told by her father that Alice was upstairs in her room, he bounded up the stairs and knocked at her door. "Alice, I have to talk to you."

She came to the door and opened it, and he went inside before she could change her mind, closing the door behind him. "Alice," he said, "Rachel just came to my office to see me. Alice," he said before she could answer that, "I want you to listen to what I have to say, because I'm only going to say it once. Rachel and I have a son whom I love very much. That does not mean I love my son's mother. I never did, and I don't now. I was attracted by her, amused by her—and I was cheated and tricked and abused by her."

He shook his head. "It so happens that right now I feel sorry for her, because she has this insane notion that if you divorce me I'll go back to her. Alice, there is no way of that happening. No way. I can't stop you from divorcing me if you insist on it. But I can tell you I'm never going back to Rachel. When I was at Berryville Rachel came to see me one day. She said if I had stayed with her instead of going back to you I wouldn't have been there in that prison. Would you like to know, Alice, what I told her? I said I would rather be in that prison than to have stayed with her. And I meant it. Alice, Rachel told me something today about you. She showed me a lab report. Darling, that's what's been bothering you, isn't it—that you can't ever have another child?"

Up until now Alice hadn't taken her eyes from his face, but now she looked down. "Yes."

"Alice, look at me." When she did he said, "Alice, I would have liked to have more children. I don't deny that. You and I have talked about it many times. But, Alice, I can live without children. It's you I can't live without. Alice, do you care what happens to me?"

There were tears in her eyes. "Yes, Steven. Of course I care."

His dark eyes were intent upon her. "Show me."

"How?"

"By coming back to me. By living with me. Alice, you're the only woman I want. Now and forever." He reached out to her. "Alice, I love you. Come to me, please."

The tears streamed down her face as she went into his arms. "Oh, Steven."

He held her close. "Darling. My darling."

She pulled far enough back to say, "I only wanted what was best for you."

"You're what's best for me," he said. "You always have been. You always will be. Will you come home with me now?"

"Yes. Oh, Steven, I love you so. I've missed you so."

And home she went with him.

The next day they flew down to his beach house on the island of Saint Croix, feeling again like honeymooners.

That same day Ada went to see Rachel. Rachel had told her about the report, and Ada said now as she took off her coat, "Your scheme backfired, Rachel."

Rachel frowned. "What scheme?"

"To get Steve to come back to you. Rachel, he isn't coming back. I tried to tell you that, but—"

Rachel cut her off. "You don't know he isn't coming back."

"Yes, I do know. He and Alice have reconciled."

"I don't believe you."

"Well, believe me or not, it's true. They reconciled last night, and today they flew down to St. Croix for a belated second honeymoon."

Rachel stared at her mother, then burst into tears.

For the next few days Rachel couldn't be consoled, but as more and more time passed she finally accepted what her mother had been trying to get her to accept for a long time—that Steve wanted and loved Alice, not her.

And besides, in spending all that time with Iris Carrington, Rachel had met Iris's father, Mackenzie Cory, who had at least as many millions as Steve had—and maybe more. . . .

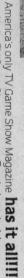

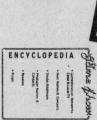